WITNESS TO REVOLUTION

Growing Up in
Williamsburg
During the
American Revolution

MICHAEL & JENNIFER CECERE

HERITAGE BOOKS
2023

HERITAGE BOOKS
AN IMPRINT OF HERITAGE BOOKS, INC.

Books, CDs, and more—Worldwide

For our listing of thousands of titles see our website
at
www.HeritageBooks.com

Published 2023 by
HERITAGE BOOKS, INC.
Publishing Division
5810 Ruatan Street
Berwyn Heights, MD 20740

Copyright © 2023 Michael and Jennifer Cecere

Cover design by Jennifer Cecere

All rights reserved. No part of this book may be reproduced or transmitted in any form or by any means, electronic or mechanical, including photocopying, recording or by any information storage and retrieval system without written permission from the author, except for the inclusion of brief quotations in a review.

International Standard Book Number
Paperbound: 978-#######

Table of Contents

Chapter 1	Have You Seen the Ghosts Yet? 1771	1
Chapter 2	Every Respectable Virginian Knows How to Dance 1771	19
Chapter 3	Families Belong Together 1771	37
Chapter 4	If We Submit, We Shall be Nothing But Slaves 1772	51
Chapter 5	Fight 'Em 1773	67
Chapter 6	I Appreciate Your Candor 1774	81
Chapter 7	We Cannot Remain Idle Spectators 1774	101
Chapter 8	Betsy Farrow 1774	113
Chapter 9	Are We Gonna Fight, Father? 1775	125
Chapter 10	Williamsburg is an Armed Camp 1775	149
Chapter 11	Independence 1776	169
Chapter 12	God Save General Washington 1776	183
Chapter 13	My God, Becca! 1777	195

Acknowledgements

There is no way I would have even attempted my first work in historical fiction without the assistance of my co-author and daughter, Jennifer Cecere Miyazaki. I may have a solid handle on the Revolutionary history of Virginia, but she knows how to write, and it was an absolute joy to work with her on this book. She made my ideas come alive with her descriptive writing and she provided fantastic story ideas as well.

Kate Metherell and her children, Cash, Lola, and Ryleigh, also deserve my heartfelt thanks for encouraging me to write this book AND providing me with valuable feedback on the drafts. I see a lot of each of you in the characters guys, and it has been a pleasure to help you with American History this year.

My friends at Colonial Williamsburg also deserve recognition for their steadfast dedication to telling America's past in an authentic manner. There is no better place in the world to inspire folks about the American Revolution than Colonial Williamsburg, and I appreciate all that the foundation and its wonderful people do. Felicity Meza-Luna at the Rockefeller Library gave me some very good advice on writing fiction that was much appreciated. The fine folks at Heritage Books were also very helpful with the book, especially Debbie Riley who edited the book. We are also grateful to Michael Simpson, Hope Trimpe and Julian Rizzi and their families for permission to use their images on the cover.

Lastly, I want to thank my wife Susan for her feedback on the book. Although History is not her thing, I am encouraged that Jenny and I have written a book that she enjoys.

About the Authors

Michael Cecere is a retired History teacher who resides in Williamsburg, Virginia with his wife, Susan. Originally from Maine, he taught high school and college level American History for thirty years in Virginia. The author of over twenty books and numerous articles on the American Revolution and Revolutionary War, he continues to research and write in retirement.

When he is not writing, Mr. Cecere volunteers and works at Colonial Williamsburg and Jamestown Settlement, sometimes as a tobacco farmer, other times as a soldier or a colonial dancer. He also participates in Revolutionary War reenactments throughout the east coast and lectures at historic sites and historical societies.

Jennifer Cecere Miyazaki is a passionate writer like her father, but until now, has kept her writing mostly to herself. She grew up in Virginia but has spent the majority of her post-university life in Tokyo, Japan, where she now resides with her husband, their dog, and soon-to-be newborn daughter. In addition to her love of writing, she enjoys teaching—particularly children—and has spent the past decade inspiring young learners to follow their dreams.

A self-identified "daddy's girl," she was beyond thrilled to work on this book with her father, who she has always admired. When she is not writing or teaching, she can be found having long-distance conversations with her family, out in nature with her dog and husband, or on the couch with a book in hand.

Glossary of Terms

Apprentice: A person who works for a skilled tradesman or tradeswoman and works for them over several years to learn the trade themselves.

Ball: A party with dancing, gaming, and fine food.

Bedchamber: A bedroom.

Capitol: The building where the government meets.

Capital: The city where the government meets.

Chamber Pots: Large pots used as a toilet.

Curtsy: A gesture of respect by bending at the knee while keeping your back straight and your hands held to your front or on the side holding your gown or petticoat (dress). Generally, only performed by women.

Dissolve the House of Burgesses: Suspend the Assembly and call for new elections.

Fowler: A smoothbore gun used to hunt birds.

Frock: A dress.

Gaming: Gambling.

Gentry: The upper class of society.

Indentured Convict Servant: A convicted criminal in Britain sent to the colonies under orders to serve as a servant for a number of years.

Inflammatory: Controversial, bound to upset people.

Loyalist: A colonist who remained devoted to the King and England.

Milliner: A person who makes and sells women's clothing and accessories such as gloves, neckerchiefs, hats, and lace.

Minuet: A very formal dance performed by one couple.

Natural Philosophy: Natural Science.

Patriot: A colonist who opposed Britain and ultimately supported independence for the colonies.

Privy / Necessary: Small buildings away from a home where the toilet was.

Public Times: Times when the House of Burgesses and the Courts gathered in Williamsburg.

Reconciliation: To settle differences and repair a damaged relationship.

Rifle: A gun with a rifled (grooved) barrel that makes its shot more accurate than a smoothbore muskets or fowler.

Subjugate: To conquer or control.

Subservient: To be forced to obey.

Tick Mattress: A large sack filled with wool or straw to sleep on.

Tory: A colonist who remained loyal to the King and England. Used interchangeably with "loyalist."

Usurped: Taken away from without permission.

Vendor: Someone who sells something.

Wager: A bet.

Historical Timeline of Important Events Prior to 1771

1763   The **Treaty of Paris** officially ends the French & Indian War.
The **Proclamation Line** is announced, forbidding any settlement west of the Appalachian Mountains until further notice.

1764   The **Sugar Act** is passed and strengthens British laws to reduce colonial smuggling.

1765   The **Stamp Act** is passed. There is now a tax on paper items in the American colonies to help pay for the enormous debt of the French & Indian War. It's the first tax on the colonists that was designed to raise revenue (money) from them.
Opposition to the Stamp Act spreads and "No taxation without representation!" is declared by colonists. Letters & petitions are sent to London in opposition and violence against British officials in the colonies occurs.

1766   Parliament repeals **the Stamp Act** and passes **the Declaratory Act**, which states that Parliament has the right to "rule over the colonies on all matters whatsoever!"

1767   Parliament passes the **Townshend Duties.** This puts tariffs on paper, paint, glass, and other goods imported from Britain. Colonists oppose these duties and claim they are a scheme to raise revenue, not regulate trade—which is what tariffs are supposed to do.

1769   Virginians adopt a **Non-importation Association** agreement to boycott British goods covered by the Townshend Duties.

1770   The **Boston Massacre** occurs. British troops fire into a crowd in Boston, killing and wounding several people. Parliament repeals the **Townshend Duties**, but leaves a tax on tea.

Introduction

The inspiration for this book occurred one day while I sat in the Visitor's Center of Colonial Williamsburg signing books and interacting with guests. I've written over twenty books since 2004, all historical non-fiction on the American Revolution. Some are biographies of Virginian officers in the war and others are histories of the Revolution and the war in general.

As I sat at the table dressed as a Revolutionary soldier with a selection of my most recent books, I happily engaged with visitors about Williamsburg, the Revolution, and my books. Inevitably, parents asked, "are any of your books appropriate for my child?"

If their child was late middle school or high school age I would reply yes, but often they were younger and the last thing I wanted to do was disappoint a new reader with a book that was too difficult for them to read, so I answered honestly and said, probably not.

After about six exchanges of this kind one morning, I had one of those Ah-ha moments. You know, when the light bulb turns on over your head.

"I'll do it," I thought. "I'll write a new book *for* kids. And I'll write it as historical fiction to make the Revolution come alive for them."

On paper it was a great idea. I live in the perfect setting, Williamsburg, Virginia. So many historical figures, George Washington, Patrick Henry, Thomas Jefferson, Richard Henry Lee, George Wythe, and on and on spent time in Williamsburg during the Revolution. And so many important decisions and events occurred there. What better setting could there be, especially since the city has been restored to appear as it did in colonial times. Talk about an inspiration to write.

My daily walks with Daisy, my dear little dog who absolutely adores walking down Duke of Gloucester Street, became brainstorming sessions for plot ideas. I already had a thorough understanding of the historical events that occurred in Williamsburg, but I needed to bring those events, and the people who experienced them, to life. Walking in Williamsburg every day and visiting the Raleigh and Wetherburn taverns, the Wythe and Randolph houses, the Capitol and Governor's Palace, and all the other historic buildings in this amazing city provided me with a wealth of ideas and detail for the book.

But there was a problem. I had never written fiction before. And perhaps even worse, I didn't read much of it either. If I was going to do this, I needed help. So, I turned to my daughter, Jennifer.

Now I admit, I could be biased, but Jenny is brilliant, especially in regards to writing. She graduated from Virginia Commonwealth University Summa Cum Laude (the highest distinction) with an English degree and has taught English to students in Japan for the last decade.

She is an outstanding writer and editor and she knows fiction, so I asked her to co-write the book with me and she agreed. Her input has been phenomenal.

I have a thorough understanding of the time period and events of the Revolution. Jenny knows how to bring a story to life through dialogue and descriptive writing. She also has a very keen sense of realism with the characters, finding just the right reaction – given their age and situation in the story – for each character.

It has been a joy for me to watch her improve my writing and add rich detail to some of the story lines. "Show Don't Tell," is the phrase she used repeatedly with me. The teacher in me wanted to tell the story as a narrator, but she insisted that the characters themselves tell as much of the story as possible, and they do.

One of the things that we hope makes this book so exciting is that most of the places described in it still exist. You can visit the Raleigh and Wetherburn taverns, the Capitol, Governor's Palace, Powder Magazine, Courthouse, Bruton Church, the College, and even the pleasant brook behind the print shop where the main characters spent so much time. Our hope is that readers of the book will visit Williamsburg and walk in the footsteps of these characters. Many were real people. The Raleigh Tavern was owned by the Southall's in the 1770's and Wetherburn's Tavern was leased by Robert Anderson for most of that decade.

As in all fiction, some liberty is taken with the characters, but authenticity to the time period is crucial, and we did our best to write a book of historical fiction that is as accurate as possible to the time period and events portrayed.

All the recognizable historical figures mentioned in the book did frequently visit Williamsburg, as well as the Raleigh and Mr. Anderson's taverns. Important events like the formation of the Committee of Correspondence and the Non-Importation Association *did* occur in the Apollo room of the Raleigh. Williamsburg was indeed turned into an armed camp in 1775-76 and there was a public ball in the Capitol to celebrate the American victory at Saratoga in November 1777.

Our hope is simple. We want readers to understand what happened in the American Revolution and why it was so important. We have divided the story into two books. The events in this first book take place between 1771 to 1777. The main characters begin as young children, ages 7 to 9 living in Williamsburg, Virginia in 1771. By the end of this book they are 13 to 15 years old and the boys are nearly old enough to serve in the war. The experience of all three characters with the Revolutionary War is the focus of the second book.

For now, we hope you enjoy this first book. It is the story of the American Revolution in Williamsburg as witnessed through the eyes of James and John Southall and Rebecca Anderson.

Chapter 1

Have You Seen the Ghosts Yet?
1771

"As I have recently entered the Raleigh Tavern, I beg leave to solicit the Customers of that House for a Continuance of their Favours, and hereby acquaint the Gentlemen who lodged there in past publick Times that their Rooms will still be kept in order to receive them. I flatter myself that I will be able to give Satisfaction; as no pains nor cost shall be spared for that end."

--- James Southall, March 7, 1771
Purdie & Dixon's *Virginia Gazette*

James and John Southall felt a twinge of sadness as they walked down the front steps of Mrs. Wetherburn's tavern in Williamsburg. The young boys were leaving the only home they had ever known.

Eight-year-old James was the older of the two. Their father first rented Wetherburn's tavern from the widow

Wetherburn in 1763 and it had been their home for the past eight years.

"I'm going to miss it," said James's seven-year-old brother John.

"We're just going across the street, you'll still see it every day," replied his brother. "Besides, everybody says the Raleigh is the best tavern in the city and father owns it now. Someone else can rent this one."

Growing up in a tavern in colonial Virginia presented both challenges and opportunities for children. Screaming babies were not something tavern guests tolerated, so the Southalls were relieved that their first born, James, was an exceptionally quiet, well-behaved child. He seemed perfectly content in his cradle as a baby and eager to learn as a toddler.

Mrs. Southall was proud of her eldest son's natural curiosity and desire to learn. She nurtured these traits with daily lessons that taught James his letters, numbers, and handwriting. As he grew older and learned mathematics and how to read, James took every opportunity he could to find a quiet spot in the tavern to read a book or a copy of the *Virginia Gazette*, the weekly newspaper. He also kept a journal.

That's not to say that James didn't enjoy the lively conversations he overheard from tavern guests. He could be social when he wanted, but oftentimes he preferred to observe—soaking up stories to record in his journal.

Conversing with guests in the tavern were activities better suited for John, who was more outgoing and social than James. Born nearly thirteen months after James, during the Christmas season of 1763, John was his older brother's opposite from the very start. Where James was a quiet and seemingly content baby, John was loud and fussy—demanding twice the attention James needed. This desire for attention never faded and he sometimes escaped the notice of his parents in the tavern and wandered up to a table full of guests to interrupt a game of cards, or dice. The guests usually found such incidents amusing, but occasionally John got ahold of the cards or dice in the middle of a wager and the person who was about to win did not always appreciate John's interference.

When he was not dropping by the gaming tables uninvited, John would sometimes solicit food from a guest's plate. Colonel George Washington nearly fell out of his chair with laughter one afternoon in 1770 when six-year-old John wandered into the club room and overheard Colonel Washington say, "This sweet bread is excellent."

John stopped in his tracks. He had never tasted sweet bread before, but knew he liked sweet things and bread so he figured it *must* be good.

John approached Colonel Washington with an expression on his face that very much said, "Can I have some?"

Colonel Washington hesitated to offer a bite, but the other gentlemen at the table encouraged him to "let the boy have a taste," so he lifted his plate toward John. With a big smile, John took a piece of what looked like fried cauliflower and popped it in his mouth.

As he chewed and swallowed the morsel, John's face contorted into a mixture of surprise and revulsion. He gagged, shook his head violently from side to side, and licked his lips, desperate to remove the foul taste from his mouth. Sweet bread was not at all what he expected! It was neither sweet, nor bread, but rather, the thymus gland of a young cow taken from its neck. John learned this later when he asked his mother about the horrible tasting cauliflower with a cruelly misleading name.

The gentlemen at the table watched John's reaction with delight and burst into laughter. Colonel Washington called out, "bring a glass of cider for the lad, he needs to wash the sweet bread down." He then turned to the gentlemen at the table and declared, "I wager that's the last sweet bread this boy ever eats," and patted John on the head.

Despite the horrible taste that lingered, John smiled at all the attention. He also resolved to be more careful about what he ate.

John's bold and often mischievous nature led to far more "corrections" with a hickory switch than James ever received. Painful as they were, the whippings occasionally provided entertainment to the tavern's guests, who watched with smirks as John twisted and turned like a fish out of water to avoid blows to his backside from his parents.

Although the nature of the two boys was very different, they were extremely close. James felt a responsibility to look out for his younger brother and they were together much of each day. John was indeed a handful to deal with, but over the years a bond developed between the two that was exceptionally strong.

In physical appearance they were so similar that John looked like a twin of James, albeit smaller. Both had brown eyes and a slight curl to their brown hair, which fell to their shoulders when not tied back. The curl was less apparent with James, who kept his hair shorter in the front and out of his eyes, while John's flopped over his eyes like "an unruly sheepdog," his mother complained.

The boys' father, James Southall, was older than most fathers with children their age. He married late in life, at age 31, but the wait was worth it. Their mother, Frances Jennings, who was just 20 when she married, was a sweet and lovely lady. Young James was their first child, born in early December 1762. John followed in late December 1763, then a daughter, Frances in late 1767. Five more siblings would follow over the next decade.

When the Southalls moved across Duke of Gloucester Street into their new home in the Raleigh Tavern in the spring of 1771, they did not do so alone. Mr. Southall brought twelve enslaved people with him—six adults and six children—all experienced at tavern work and every person his property under Virginia law.

There was Flora and her two young daughters. Flora cooked for the Southalls and their guests while her daughters worked by her side. They helped where they could and watched and learned their mother's skills in the kitchen. Their enslaved father, William, was a valet—a personal servant—to Mr. Thomas Nelson Jr. of Yorktown. Mr. Nelson visited the Raleigh often, which gave William a chance to see his wife and children. These visits, however, were far too short and infrequent.

Flora and her daughters worked every day from early morning until late afternoon in the kitchen and slept upstairs in a loft. Most southerners, including the Southall family, preferred to have their kitchens in a separate building—not at all connected to the main house if possible. This was to keep the heat and flies found in every colonial kitchen out of their home.

The scullery work of cleaning pots, pans and dishes fell to Dinah, who was 14 years old. She was separated from her parents as a baby and purchased by Mr. Southall just a year earlier in an auction in front of the Raleigh Tavern. When she was not washing dishes, Dinah helped with the laundry, which was done at least twice a week and sometimes more when the tavern was busy. She also slept in the loft above the kitchen. William worked in the stable at the back of the lot where he cared for the family's two horses and those brought by the tavern's visitors. He also tended to the grounds of the tavern as well as the building itself. He slept above the stable in a loft.

Fanny and Kate were housekeepers who kept the entire tavern clean and presentable—an endless chore in such a large establishment with so many guests coming and going. Kate's two young daughters helped their mother while her twelve-year-old son fetched wood and water, started the daily fires throughout the tavern every morning, and occasionally—and with great reluctance—helped his sisters empty and clean chamber pots. He also helped William in the stables. Kate's enslaved husband was held by Mr. James Anderson, a blacksmith whose shop was across the street just a few lots up from the Raleigh.

Tom and George, two enslaved brothers in their early twenties, served as waiters inside the tavern. Both were taken from their mother and sold when they were very young and had no recollection of her. Mr. Southall purchased both boys from Mrs. Wetherburn in 1763 when he leased her tavern. They had served her as waiters and continued to do so for Mr. Southall.

The enslaved people who worked inside the tavern were provided with better clothing than those who worked away from the house, but they had far less privacy. The housekeepers and waiters in the tavern were seen regularly by the Southalls and their guests and thus had to look presentable. They also had to be ready to serve at a moment's notice—day or night. As a result, they slept on bedding laid out in the hallway upstairs—always within earshot of Mr. or Mrs. Southall.

In addition to the enslaved people who worked at the Raleigh, Mr. Southall hired a bar keeper named William Drinkard to manage his valuable supply of liquor and serve as an assistant. Mr. Drinkard was a quiet man who always had a serious look on his face and he lived in a small room at the Raleigh behind the front stairs. Mr. Southhall kept a small office next to the bar keeper's room and the Southalls had a large private room for themselves next to the public dining room.

The Southall's former residence across the street, Wetherburn's Tavern, did not stay vacant very long after the family left. Robert Anderson, his wife Elizabeth, and their daughter Rebecca—just two months shy of her seventh birthday—moved into the tavern the same week that the Southalls moved out.

Robert Anderson had managed a small tavern on the other side of town near the college and he leapt at the chance to rent Wetherburn's when it became available. Its closer location to the capitol and reputation as one of Williamsburg's finer taverns offered the Andersons a chance for greater profit.

Like the Raleigh across the street, Anderson's tavern had a room devoted to public dining and a number of bed chambers upstairs. It also had a club room for gaming or private dining and a large ballroom. The family themselves stayed in two small rooms in the back of the tavern.

Robert Anderson's daughter, Rebecca, was just a few months younger than John Southall, but her disposition was closer to his older brother James. She had her mother's red hair and her father's sparkling blue eyes. Her demeanor was pleasant and cheerful, but there was a seriousness to her that made her seem dependable, yet a bit reserved.

James and John were barely acquainted with Rebecca before she moved into Wetherburn's Tavern. They saw her only on Sundays at church, but always greeted her politely with a slight bow and a muttered "good day." She of course replied in kind and curtsied. Because they lived on opposite ends of town, however, they never spoke beyond such greetings. But that changed on March 9, 1771—the day Rebecca and her family moved into Wetherburn's Tavern across from the Raleigh.

It was James who uncharacteristically approached Rebecca first when he saw her sitting on the front steps of his old home. Something about her piqued his curiosity. Her expression, perhaps, as she gazed wistfully at the clouds. He thought he recognized a kindred spirit in her, a fellow introvert. He walked across the street and bowed solemnly to her from the foot of the steps, removing his hat.

"James Southall at your service," he said.

Rebecca had risen to her feet as he approached, nervous at the impending encounter. She curtsied as formally as she could in response. "A pleasure to meet you, sir."

Before she could introduce herself, John burst upon the scene. He had been inside the Raleigh when his brother started across the street and followed twenty paces behind. Hurrying to catch up, he nearly knocked James down when he arrived. John steadied James by the shoulder, then bowed to Rebecca *without* removing his hat and said very seriously, "John Southall."

A bemused smile flashed across her face. "Pleased to meet you both," she replied as she curtsied again. "I am Rebecca. Rebecca Anderson."

Both boys nodded in acknowledgement and then John took over. "So, how do you like our old house? Have you seen any ghosts yet? It *is* haunted you know. Me and James heard one just a week ago before we moved out."

"James and I," corrected James, prompting a slight giggle from Rebecca.

"How do you like all the room you have now?" continued John, undeterred by the correction. "I'll wager it's twice as big as the place you moved from. What do you think of the Great Room? All the best people have danced there, and we've watched 'em. Now they'll have to come over to the Raleigh and dance in our Apollo Room. It's the fanciest room in the city."

"Except for the governor's ballroom," corrected James again.

John shot his brother a pointed look and stepped closer to Rebecca. "Anyway. The ghost is…"

Heat prickled James's cheeks. This was no way to speak to a lady. Conversations were meant to be balanced, but Rebecca couldn't get a word in. Instead, she stood leaning slightly back, listening politely, her hands cupped in front as if she were about to curtsey again and remove herself from John's interrogation.

Let the poor girl speak, thought James to himself. And then, with unexpected boldness, he interrupted John. "Do you have any brothers or sisters, Miss Anderson?"

Startled by the sound of James's voice, Rebecca looked down at her feet and whispered, "No, I'm an only child. My parents want more children but," she looked up at James with a sad smile, "the Lord has not seen fit to bless them yet."

"What about your people?" resumed John, tossing a scowl at his brother for interrupting him. "How many slaves did you bring with you?"

"Well," Rebecca started, pausing to count in her head, "we brought Sally and her two girls to cook and work in the kitchen, Jane and her daughter to keep house, and John to–"

"John! You have a slave named John?" the younger brother scoffed. "Well, I don't like that. Not one bit."

Placing his hands on his hips and his shoulders defiantly back, John declared, "We'll have to call him something else."

Rebecca straightened. "He's very nice," she responded firmly, "and he's been called John a lot longer than you, so if anyone needs to change names, I'm afraid it should be you."

Both boys were taken aback by such daring words from the previously meek girl before them. Inspired by her spirit, James proposed a solution. "What if we call your John Big John and we call this John," he motioned toward his brother, "Little John?"

Rebecca gave a small laugh before clasping her hands over her mouth in an attempt to hide her smile. John was less amused.

"No, no, no! *That* will not do!" But James and Rebecca's laughter was contagious, and John soon found himself smiling too. He crossed his arms and looked at his brother. "Well, I guess I can share my name with him. Provided he is a true and honest servant."

"Oh, he is, he is," insisted Rebecca. "He's been with us all my life and for much of my father's too."

Just then the front door opened and Big John appeared. He was indeed big and appeared to be the same age as the boys' father. "Miss Rebecca, your mama is looking for you, you best come in now."

Rebecca curtsied to the boys. "Pleased to meet you both," she said as she turned and scurried inside.

"Good day, gentlemen," Big John nodded to them and closed the door.

James and John remained on the porch for a moment before crossing the street and returning to the Raleigh.

"What did you think of her?" John asked. "She didn't say much, did she?"

"How could she?" replied James, "you talked enough for all of us."

"I did not!"

"When you ask a question, it is customary to pause to let the other person answer. But you just bombarded her with question after question."

"I paused!" John insisted. James just smiled and shook his head as they walked into the Raleigh to clean up for dinner. He knew it was useless to try and convince John otherwise.

Across the street in Mr. Anderson's new tavern, Rebecca sat down to dinner with her parents. They had spent the day settling into Mrs. Wetherburn's building and were still at least a week away from opening to the public.

"How was your day, Rebecca?" asked her father once they were all seated.

"I met the boys that lived here before us," she answered. "They said our tavern is haunted."

"Do you believe them?" asked her mother.

"Indeed not, I think they, or I should say John, the younger one, was just trying to frighten me."

Her mother's eyes narrowed. "That's not very kind of him."

Rebecca worried that she had given her parents the wrong impression of the boys, especially James, who had indeed been kind to her.

"I think it was just a jest mother. They were actually quite polite."

"How old are they?" asked her father.

"I'm not sure," replied Rebecca. "James is certainly older than John, but I don't know their ages."

"Judging by how well their father managed this tavern," said Mr. Anderson, "I expect they are fine lads. I wouldn't worry too much about a jest."

Rebecca glanced around the room. "Yes, the boys seemed quite proud of this tavern."

"And rightly so," declared her father. "Mr. Southall is well regarded. I hope to build a similar reputation here."

"I'm sure you will, dear," replied Mrs. Anderson.

"Yes, of course you will, Father," added Rebecca.

Anderson's (Wetherburn) Tavern

Raleigh Tavern

Chapter 2

Every Respectable Virginian
Knows How to Dance
1771

Tavernkeepers in Virginia were required by law to provide guests with food, drink, and lodging at fixed prices. The main meal of each day was dinner, served sometime between 2 to 3 o'clock in the afternoon. Virginians often ate a light meal in the evening called supper—usually leftovers from dinner—and started each day with breakfast in the morning.

Tavern prices were set by the county courts. For one shilling a guest at the Raleigh could dine on a dish of meat, poultry, or fish—whichever was offered that day. It was sometimes left over from the day before. A vegetable dish of whatever was in season and available was also offered, and some bread—typically cornbread. Drinks, ranging from small beer and cider to wine and rum, could be purchased by the glass or bottle.

Overnight lodging for guests and care for their horses were also offered at rates set by the courts. The Raleigh charged 7½ pence to lodge overnight, and an additional 7½ was charged to stable a horse overnight. This did not mean, however, that guests received their own bedchamber or bed. The fixed rate was just for a sleeping space *inside* the tavern. It was very common for two men to share one bed and several others to sleep in the same room on the floor during busy times of the year.

If a guest wanted a bed or entire bedchamber to themselves, they paid significantly more. Tavernkeepers were free to negotiate prices for such private arrangements. The same was true for private gatherings at the tavern. Mr. Southall would often rent one of the Raleigh's smaller rooms to a party of gentlemen for a private dinner or an evening of gaming (gambling). This was called clubbing and the gentlemen would typically split the bill amongst themselves at the end of the evening.

The Raleigh offered several private club rooms to guests—for the right price—and was the preferred tavern of many gentlemen in Virginia. It was thus often crowded with guests, especially during Public Times when the House of Burgesses and the courts were in session.

During such times the Southalls squeezed their entire family into their private room next to the dining room.

They wanted to leave as much space as possible for paying customers, who were almost always men.

John noticed this tendency and asked his mother one night why so few ladies stayed at the tavern.

"Well dear," replied Mrs. Southall, "it's just not proper for ladies to share a bed with strangers the way men do at taverns."

"I should say so," declared Mr. Southall. "A proper lady would never share her bed with anyone other than her husband."

"Besides," added James, "Ladies could never tolerate the smell of some who stay here. *I* can barely tolerate it!"

Mr. and Mrs. Southall laughed at that.

John gave a little chuckle at his brother's remark as well, but was still curious for answers. "So," he said, "where do the ladies stay?"

"Well," replied Mrs. Southall, "if they do travel, they stay with family or friends or sometimes in a private room of a respectable boarding house. But in truth, women do not travel nearly as much as men do. They have little reason to."

John thought for a moment. "But mother, *you* stay at a tavern every night. How do you tolerate it?"

Mrs. Southall's eyes widened as a snort of laughter threatened to escape her, but before she could answer, Mr. Southall patted her hand. "Your mother is a strong woman, stronger than most. I couldn't manage without her, so she has no choice. She has to stay."

Mrs. Southall squeezed her husband's arm. "Thank you, dear," she smiled. She then turned to John. "I can manage here because we have our own private quarters that we share. So, I never have to sleep next to a stranger. Just a whiny baby or," she poked at John playfully, "a dirty little boy. Which reminds me, it's time to wash up for bed!"

Mrs. Southall's explanation highlighted one of the challenges of raising a family in a tavern. Personal living space was limited and cramped. James and John were old enough to dine with their parents every day, but the younger children ate earlier in the private quarters, attended by their mother. James, John, and their parents dined at a small table in the public dining room. Mr. Southall's enslaved men, Tom and George, served them dinner every day at 2:00 p.m., an hour before the tavern guests were served. The Southalls almost always ate whatever was served to their guests. They dined faster than most people in Virginia—rushing to finish before 3 p.m. so that they could attend to their guests.

When business was slow or when the guests had finished dinner and the dining room was empty—usually by 6:00 p.m.—the Southalls took advantage of the extra space and used it for themselves. On most evenings, James and John slept on bedding on the floor of the dining room. Their four-year-old sister Frances wanted to join them, but Mrs. Southall said she was still too young. Sometimes in the summer the boys slept upstairs where all the guest bedchambers were. The beds were a nice change from the tick mattresses stuffed with wool that they typically slept on, but the summer weather usually made the rooms upstairs uncomfortably hot.

The grandest room of all in the Raleigh was the Apollo Room, located toward the back of the tavern. Spacious enough to hold a hundred people, the room was used for grand balls, receptions, lectures, and meetings. The family never had occasion to use this room themselves—it was instead used almost every night for gaming or private functions. Occasionally, the room was used for much more important activities.

Two years before Mr. Southall bought the Raleigh, Virginia's royal governor, Lord Botetourt, became angry with the House of Burgesses for criticizing the British Parliament. He dissolved the House of Burgesses and forbid the burgesses to meet in the capitol. Instead of returning to their homes, however, many of the burgesses met in the Apollo Room of the Raleigh to discuss how to respond.

Colonel George Washington proposed a plan drawn up by his neighbor, George Mason, to boycott (no longer buy) certain British goods that Parliament had placed taxes on. This was a bold action for Virginia's representatives to take in 1769—some even called it disloyal and treasonous. But the boycott likely convinced Parliament to repeal most of the taxes (except the one on tea) in 1770. James and John were proud that this Non-Importation Association of 1769 was drafted in the Apollo Room of their father's tavern.

Still, the operation of the Raleigh and Mr. Anderson's tavern across the street were not matters that concerned James, John and Rebecca too greatly. They focused instead on their studies at home (reading, writing, and arithmetic), as well as their chores and dance lessons. Rebecca enjoyed dancing immensely, but it was just another chore to the boys.

"Every respectable Virginian knows how to dance," Mrs. Southall insisted, "and my children *will* be respectable!"

While James did not particularly like the dance lessons, he was quite good. Precision was something he always appreciated, and that precision was mirrored in the way he moved across the dance floor. The various steps and movements did nothing but confuse John, however, and he was frustrated with every lesson.

Prior to their move to the Raleigh, and Rebecca's move across the street, all three children were taught how to dance at home by their mothers. The increasing demands of the new taverns, however, left them less time to focus on the children's lessons, so each mother turned to a dancing master to pick up where they had left off.

Mrs. Southall and Mrs. Anderson both engaged the services of Mr. William Fearson, a stern instructor, aptly named. A violinist accompanied Mr. Fearson for each lesson. At first an indentured convict servant named Andrew Franks played dance tunes for the lessons, but he ran away that summer, so Mr. Fearson rented an enslaved boy everyone called Fiddler Billy from Edward Nicholson. Mr. Nicholson received four pounds for Billy's services as a fiddler. Billy received nothing.

The Southalls and Andersons paid Mr. Fearson two pounds a year to teach English country dancing to their children. This was half his usual rate, which he reduced in exchange for the use of an assembly room for a large group session twice a month in the Raleigh and once a month at Anderson's. Mr. Fearson was permitted to invite as many students as he wished to attend the group lesson. There were also individual lessons each Wednesday for all three children, which began in late March. These lasted several hours a session and were held in the children's homes.

Rebecca's lesson was in the morning and from the very start she excelled at the graceful movements and steps of English country dancing.

"Very good my dear," Mr. Fearson repeated during Rebecca's lessons as she mastered another dance step or movement with ease. 'Wonderful, wonderful!" Fearson exclaimed constantly throughout her lessons. Needless to say, Rebecca enjoyed everything about dancing.

Mr. Fearson rarely expressed the same sentiments to the Southall boys during their private lesson in the afternoon. The pair were instructed together at the Raleigh each Wednesday afternoon before dinner, and the comments overheard from Mr. Fearson in their sessions sounded more like ones heard in the army rather than a dance lesson.

"One, two, three, four—listen to the music, boys! You're out of step with the music!" Mr. Fearson would shout over and over again. "Concentrate! Stop daydreaming and remember the movements!"

To John, the wide variety of dance steps and movements were a blur. "Cast down, cast up, cross over, cloverleaf turn, allemande, rights and lefts, hays—the steps and movements went on and on, each as confusing as the next. James did better, but still never managed to impress Mr. Fearson. The boys found their lessons frustrating and tedious, but they happened every Wednesday and most Fridays nonetheless.

It was during the first Friday session in the Apollo Room of the Raleigh in mid-April that Rebecca and the boys next met. Five students joined James, John, and Rebecca in this late morning session—three girls and a boy. Mr. Fearson was disappointed. The lesson was open, for a fee, to anyone who wished to dance—not just his current students—so he had hoped for a stronger turnout. *Perhaps next week*, he thought.

This was the first opportunity Rebecca had to dance with someone other than her mother or father. Mr. Fearson reviewed the different dance movements they were to use that day and the children practiced them several times before Mr. Fearson decided they were ready. "Let us begin with the dancing. Everyone find a partner."

All the children stood right where they were in the middle of the room, avoiding eye contact with their instructor and each other. Mr. Fearson sighed and took charge.

"Mr. Southhall, stand here," he said to John, pointing to a spot near the fiddler. "Miss Anderson, you stand across from him. Mr. Southall," he said to James this time, "you stand next to your brother and Miss Powell, you stand across from him."

Two lines began to form facing each other extending away from the fiddler. "Mr. Prentis, you stand here," continued Mr. Fearson, placing the lad next to James. "And Miss Craig, you go across from him." The only ones left were Mr. Hornsby's two daughters, who were placed at the end and instructed to dance with each other.

Mr. Fearson took his position next to the fiddler and announced, "We shall dance 'Hole in the Wall' first." Rebecca beamed. She liked this dance—it was easy and elegant. John, on the other hand, groaned. He thought it was slow—not that it mattered much because he only remembered half the movements.

Rebecca flinched at John's grimace. "What's wrong?"

"Oh nothing," lied John.

Mr. Fearson had everyone walk the dance through one progression to see all the movements, then had them return to place and told the fiddler to play the song five times through.

In English country dancing, couples always honored their partner with a bow or curtsy before each dance. When the fiddler began, Rebecca curtsied very formally, but John gave a halfhearted bow. *How rude*, Rebecca thought as she spun away from the line and walked down the outside past the next couple, just as the dance called for. She was supposed to meet John—who should have done the same thing on his side—in the middle of the two lines of dancers, but he had fallen behind the music because he had turned the wrong way.

Good lord, thought Rebecca, as she waited impatiently for John to catch up. When he finally arrived, she grabbed his hand and led him quickly up the middle, back to their proper place to catch up with the music. She gestured to John to stay put while the second couple performed the same movement in reverse.

The third movement of the dance called for John to switch places diagonally with the girl next to Rebecca, but of course, he didn't remember that, so when Miss Powell moved toward John, he just stood there befuddled. Rebecca waved at him to move and change places and he finally caught on. She then gracefully changed places with James, who had an expression of intense concentration on his face. The two couples all took hands and circled left halfway around. The first couple, Rebecca and John, then cast around the second couple again, but stayed in their new place while James and Miss Powell moved up into the first spot.

That was one rotation, or progression, of the dance. There were four more to go and Rebecca hoped that John would be better the next time through.

He wasn't.

John forgot that English country dancing was meant to be social and that after each progression everyone danced with a new couple. Constantly a step or two behind the music, John moved like a confused old man, pushed and pulled from spot to spot.

This is an easy dance, thought Rebecca. *How in the world will he dance the harder ones?*

The music mercifully came to an end after five progressions and the children were instructed to find a new dance partner.

James stepped up to Rebecca and bowed formally. "Miss Anderson, will you do me the honor of the next dance?"

Rebecca smiled. *This is more like it,* she thought. "It would be a pleasure," she said with a curtsey.

The next dance, "Well Hall", was similar to the first in pace. Despite his nerves, James danced it flawlessly. When it ended, Rebecca enthusiastically complimented him.

"That was wonderful, Mr. Southall. I was afraid perhaps you and your brother had not had many lessons yet, but I can see I was mistaken."

James smiled and gave a slight bow. "Every Wednesday afternoon, Miss Anderson."

"Well, they have certainly made an impression on you," said Rebecca, who thought to herself, *but not so much on your brother.*

Over the course of the next two hours, the students danced five dances and then danced them all again. Everyone was tired by the end of the session, but Mr. Fearson was, for the most part, pleased with what he saw.

"We shall all meet at Miss Anderson's home next week," he announced just before dismissing the students. "And I shall see each of you at your own homes before that."

The tension disappeared from John's body once the lesson ended. He turned to Rebecca as she was about to leave. "So, have you seen any ghosts yet?" he asked.

Rebecca crossed her arms. "Ghosts aren't real," she replied sharply.

John reeled backwards. Why did she seem so upset with him? "Well… I think we saw one at our—your—place once," he stammered. "But it could have been my imagination."

"It was," said James, who had walked up to hear the last bit of conversation. He loved his brother but had to admit seeing John look so bewildered was amusing. "Miss

Anderson," he said, turning his attention to her, "are you all settled into the tavern now?"

"Yes, thank you. We've been settled for a while. I like it a lot. And you? Are you all settled here?"

"Yes," replied James, "we settled in after the first week."

John stared at the two of them as they smiled at each other, feeling somehow as if he had been forgotten. He centered himself between them. "So, what do you think about this room?" he spun about, arms extended. "It's called the Apollo Room. Impressive, isn't it? You should see it when it's full of gentlemen."

Rebecca glanced around the room, her face as still as stone. "Yes, I am quite impressed," she said dully before refocusing her attention on James, her smile restored. "Thank you for dancing with me, Mr. Southall. You dance very well."

James's cheeks reddened. "Thank you, Miss Anderson," he said with a bow. "I was just trying to keep up with you."

John huffed loudly, upset at being ignored. "Have I done something to offend you, Miss Anderson?" he blurted out.

Rebecca fixed her gaze on him, her eyes cool. "Well," she said, "if you must know, you danced like a barbarian."

"A barbarian!" John gasped.

"Yes, a *barbarian.* Your manners were atrocious. You clearly did not want to dance with me."

"With *you?*"

"Yes."

James let out a laugh and received a stern look from both. He cleared his throat and came to John's defense. "I think you should know, Miss Anderson, that—" but before he finished John cut him off.

"Miss Anderson, I didn't want to dance with *anyone,*" exclaimed John. "I hate dancing."

Rebecca blinked.

"It's true," James insisted.

There was a moment of awkward silence before it was broken by laughter. Rebecca's hands flew to her mouth instantly, embarrassed by not only the sudden sound of her laughter, but her assumption. "Oh, I see," she said. "I thought… I thought—"

"You saw for yourself," James declared, "why would someone that moves like *that* enjoy dancing?"

"As if you're so much better!" John shot back.

Now Rebecca and James were both laughing. "You *are* quite terrible," she said to John between breaths.

John watched the two laugh at his expense. He waited for the anger to come, but it never did. For some reason all he felt was relief. A grin broke across his face. "I suppose I *am* pretty bad," he conceded.

"You truly are!" they chuckled.

"But James isn't much better!" John cried, in a last-ditch attempt to soften the blow to his dancing reputation.

James clapped his brother on his shoulder. "No, I'm not," he agreed.

John let out a sigh and gave one last look around the Apollo Room. "I'm just glad it's all over," he said.

Smiles still on their faces, James and Rebecca nodded.

Gatherings like these occurred almost every week and as they did, James, John, and Rebecca became more than acquaintances—they became friends.

Duke of Gloucester Street

Chapter 3

Families Belong Together
1771

Business at Williamsburg's taverns was slower than normal during the first half of 1771. This was largely because several sessions of the House of Burgesses were postponed. A year earlier Lord Botetourt—the royal governor—died, and his replacement, John Murray—the 4th Earl of Dunmore—had yet to arrive. Political matters were thus suspended as the colony awaited its new governor.

Fortunately for Williamsburg's tavernkeepers, people still traveled to the city for business and court sessions. All felony criminal cases in Virginia, which were punishable by death, were tried in the General Court in Williamsburg. Trials were held in the courtroom of the capitol building in April, June, October, and December.

The new James City County courthouse across from the gunpowder magazine also held county court sessions every month to settle local disputes and minor crimes. These sessions drew people to the taverns, but not nearly as many as the number who visited when the House of Burgesses met.

Although her parents were disappointed that the tavern business had slowed, Rebecca was thrilled when one particular guest visited their tavern in the spring. Colonel George Washington, hero of the late war with the French, visited Williamsburg on business in May and stopped at Mr. Anderson's tavern twice, first to eat supper and the second time to spend an evening gaming.

It was the Anderson's first encounter with Colonel Washington. They were all familiar with his service in the late war against the French and their Native American allies and were very impressed by his tall figure and gentlemanly conduct in their tavern.

Although he spoke the least of all the gentlemen at his table, he complimented Rebecca on her pretty frock and asked her age when she entered the dining room.

"I am seven next week, sir," replied Rebecca with a curtsey. "And how old are you?"

Colonel Washington smiled at her boldness. "Well, a good deal older than that," he chuckled. "You very much remind me of my stepdaughter Patsy when she was seven. You are certainly just as pretty as she was then."

Rebecca beamed in response. "How old is she now?"

Before Colonel Washington could answer, Rebecca's father shooed her away from the table and out of the room, embarrassed by her intrusion. "Apologies for my daughter, Colonel."

"Nonsense, your charming daughter is a delight," insisted Colonel Washington. "Please tell her my Patsy is now 15 years old, and that I wish her a very happy seventh birthday."

Rebecca was disappointed that she did not get to visit with Colonel Washington on his return to the tavern two days later. He spent the evening playing cards and dice in the large assembly room. Her parents believed that such entertainment was not appropriate for children, so Rebecca remained in the family quarters the entire evening, as she did after every dinner.

Colonel Washington also visited the Raleigh Tavern during his stay in Williamsburg. He dined one afternoon with Richard Henry Lee and his cousin, Henry Lee, and returned the next evening to gamble until nearly midnight with several gentlemen—including Virginia's treasurer, Robert Carter Nicholas.

Mr. Southall did not hold the same beliefs as the Andersons about allowing children in the gaming rooms. He desired that James, at only eight years old, spend as much time around the gentlemen of Virginia as he could.

Mr. Southall had risen far in society and was now a very successful tavernkeeper. He hoped to rise even further and wanted the same for his sons. He believed that once they were mature enough, a healthy amount of interaction with the most influential people in the colony would be to their advantage. Any interaction, however, should be on the terms of the influential people—not at the whims of his young sons.

Both James and John saw Colonel Washington when he dined privately with several other gentlemen at the Raleigh in May. James stood quiet and respectful in a corner of the front club room, ready to complete any errand requested by the gentlemen.

John noticed Colonel Washington by chance when he wandered into the private room midway through Washington's dinner. James saw his brother enter, but could do nothing to stop him because he was on the other side of the room. When John entered, he fixed straight upon Colonel Washington. He walked toward him and, ever the type to get straight to the point, asked directly, "Colonel, sir, did you ever kill any Indians in the war?"

Colonel Washington was taken aback by the question and leaned back in his chair. "Why hello lad," he said, "had any sweet bread lately?" The men at the table chuckled, familiar with the story. John's face reddened, but he did not want to appear embarrassed in front of the Colonel and did his best to hold eye contact. Colonel Washington grew serious and looked hard at John, who was still waiting for an answer. "Well son, bad things happen in war, very bad things. I don't honestly know if I killed anyone—Indian or French—in the war. I certainly hope not. But if I did, I take no pleasure in it."

John did not expect this answer and stood puzzled before Colonel Washington. It was then that his father entered the room and noticed him. Horrified that John was disturbing his important guests, Mr. Southall rushed over and snatched John off the ground, apologizing for the interruption.

With John's past incidents in mind, Mr. Southall decided his seven-and-a-half-year-old son was not mature enough to tend to guests in either the dining or gaming rooms.

So, when Colonel Washington returned to the tavern the next night for an evening of gaming only James took a position in the corner of the Apollo Room until nightfall, once again ready to serve. He interacted little with the guests, smiling occasionally when one caught his gaze, but mostly he watched and listened and learned how Virginian gentlemen talked and acted.

Less than three weeks after Colonel Washington's visit to Williamsburg, a terrible flood swept down Virginia's rivers. Hundreds of people died and those who survived lost much of their livestock and crops.

Thousands of barrels of tobacco stored in warehouses along the rivers and creeks were also destroyed. Tobacco was the principal cash crop and main source of income for most Virginians, so the loss of their tobacco meant financial ruin for many families.

The House of Burgesses met in an emergency session in July to provide some relief to the victims of this natural disaster. All the tavernkeepers in Williamsburg benefitted from this unexpected surge of people to Williamsburg in the summer, which was usually the slowest time of year for the city. Virginia's leaders learned long ago to avoid summer sessions in Williamsburg—the season for heat, insects, and fevers. So, the July session of the House of Burgesses was an unexpected and pleasant surprise to the Southalls, Andersons, and Williamsburg's other tavernkeepers.

James did what he could to help his parents with this welcome rush of business. He mostly ran errands for guests, retrieving a forgotten item in a bedchamber or delivering a message to someone in the next room or across the street.

In August, Rebecca witnessed a spectacle in front of the Raleigh Tavern that sickened her. It had long been the practice to hold public auctions in front of the Raleigh whenever anyone wished to sell their property. Land, buildings, personal items, and enslaved people were sold to the highest bidder at these auctions.

The Southall boys had seen dozens of auctions during their time at Wetherburn's tavern, so when 50 enslaved men, women, and children were offered for sale in front of their new home, they thought little of it. They were with Rebecca on the front steps of her father's tavern when the auction began.

Unlike the Southall brothers, Rebecca had never seen a slave auction before. She had lived on the other side of town, so when she watched two young, enslaved children auctioned off and torn away from their distraught mother's arms she thought immediately, *this is wrong!* Tears welled in her eyes as she watched their mother plead for her babies. Rebecca dashed down the steps and then up the street, away from the auction, unable to watch the cruelty any longer.

James and John were surprised by Rebecca's reaction. They had seen such scenes dozens of times. Sure, it was sad, but they assumed the slave mother and children would soon get over their separation.

Rebecca is just too sentimental, they thought. *She doesn't understand how the world works.* It never occurred to them that the enslaved children felt the same way about their mother as *they* felt about their own mother. The boys had always been told, and so had come to believe, that slaves were different from white people. But Rebecca's reaction to the auction made the boys question that belief for the first time.

They followed after her. Turning down a side street, they found her crouched under a tree, her hands furiously swiping away tears. They approached slowly, unsure of what to say to comfort her.

Rebecca broke the silence. "That was awful," she cried.

The boys exchanged a glance, still unsure of what to say.

Rebecca stared up at them, her face bright red. "Families belong together," she said. "What if you were taken from your mother?"

"Well, that would never happ—" John started, but a swift jab from James stopped him.

"It would be awful," said James, joining Rebecca on the ground. John joined shortly after, the three friends sitting in silence until Rebecca had calmed down enough to head back home.

The heartbreaking auctions continued regularly in front of the Raleigh, a foul blight on colonial society but a practice long accepted by those who depended on slave labor to maintain their comfortable lifestyle.

In late September, Virginia's new governor, Lord Dunmore, arrived from New York. James, John, and Rebecca stood along Duke of Gloucester Street with most of the townsfolk to wave as he passed in his carriage. They caught a glimpse of the governor, but only a glimpse.

Duke of Gloucester Street

A week later, however, James had a direct encounter with the new governor. Williamsburg's leaders held a fine dinner and evening of entertainment for Governor Dunmore at the Raleigh. James stood quietly along the wall of the Apollo Room and watched as numerous toasts were offered in honor of the King, the royal family, the governor, and the rights of Englishmen.

One newspaper reported that the day was, "spent in Mirth and Sociability," and James agreed. As for Governor Dunmore, he struck James as a very genteel man, but with an explosive temper. Sort of how he imagined King Henry VIII to be two centuries earlier.

Governor Dunmore must have been impressed with the Raleigh because in late October he arranged for two celebrations on the same evening—one at his residence in the Governor's Palace and the other at the Raleigh Tavern. The occasion was the anniversary of the ascension of King George III to the throne. "The city was handsomely illuminated," reported the newspapers, "and plenty of liquor given to the population," all presumably paid for by Governor Dunmore.

At the close of 1771, James and John grew a year older. James turned nine in early December and John turned eight just after Christmas.

The Christmas season was a joyous time in Virginia filled with delicious food and drink, caroling, dancing, and laughter. It spanned twelve days, beginning on Christmas Day, with the firing of muskets into the air to mark the occasion. Most attended church on Christmas Day and many offered Christmas boxes, usually gifts of money, to their slaves, servants, and hired help.

Over the twelve days of Christmas, families hosted dances and other gatherings and there was plenty of festive food, drink, music, and song. The taverns were not as busy with overnight guests as during public times when the burgesses and courts met, but both the Raleigh Tavern and Anderson's tavern hosted balls during the Christmas season, and the children found such affairs magical. John claimed in jest that all the fun was meant in part to celebrate his own birthday, too.

The ball at the Raleigh occurred several days after Christmas. It was held in the Apollo Room and the two rooms adjoining it. James watched the first few hours of the ball from his usual position in a corner of the Raleigh.

John was not allowed to attend and was confined to the private quarters because even the public dining room was used by guests.

"But my birthday is tomorrow," complained John. "Surely eight is old enough to attend some of the ball."

"Old enough for some," replied his father with a stern look, leaving the rest of his point unsaid.

John let the matter rest and relied on his brother for a detailed description of the ball.

"There were three musicians, two fiddlers and a flutist," whispered James to his brother when he turned in for bed late that evening. "They played English and Scottish country dances the whole time, no minuets at all."

"That's because they wanted to have fun," said John, who was no fan of the formal minuet style of dance. "So, who was there?"

"I saw Mr. Nicholas, Mr. Wythe, Mr. Harrison, Mr. Blair, Mr. Digges, and Mr. Nelson. And all of their wives. I think Mr. Digges brought his son and daughter, and I know Mr. Nicholas's oldest sons danced too."

"What about Speaker Randolph and his brother?" asked John about Peyton Randolph, the Speaker of the House of Burgesses and John Randolph, the Attorney

General. The Randolphs were the most prominent family in Williamsburg, so their attendance would have been notable.

James shook his head. "I didn't see either of them."

John was disappointed, but still yearned for more details. "Who else did you see that we know?"

"A lot of our neighbors and—"

Just then the door opened and their mother peeked in.

"Shhhhhhh," she whispered with one finger to her lips. "Go to sleep, you'll wake the others." She closed the door quietly and returned to her duties.

John lifted himself upon his elbows, eager to continue talking, but James—ever the dutiful one—said, "We must do as mother says. Go to sleep John," and turned his back to him.

John sighed, *killjoy*, he thought as he closed his eyes and drifted off to sleep.

Chapter 4

If We Submit, We Shall Be Nothing But Slaves
1772

In February 1772 the House of Burgesses met in Williamsburg for two full months. Williamsburg's taverns were packed with burgesses and visitors who had business before the Assembly. James kept busy the entire time, greeting and helping guests while watching the steady merriment that occurred nightly within the Raleigh.

Colonel Washington spent a few evenings in March gaming at both Mr. Southall's and Mr. Anderson's taverns. Speaker Randolph and his brother John, along with Patrick Henry, Thomas Jefferson, Richard Henry Lee, Edmund Pendleton, and George Wythe also visited the taverns regularly—as did many other members of the House of Burgesses.

Some gentlemen, such as Colonel William Byrd of Westover, a member of the governor's council, spent nearly every evening at the Raleigh. Byrd was a notorious gambler, ready to bet on almost any outcome, and the Raleigh Tavern was his favorite spot.

When James described some of the absurd bets Colonel Byrd made, John rushed to Byrd's defense. He quite admired the man's confidence. "He sounds like he is afraid of nothing. He must be very wealthy."

"Not from gambling," James jeered. "He makes foolish wagers all the time. It's a wonder he isn't bankrupt."

John witnessed some of these bets in the spring of 1772 after he finally convinced his father to let him join James in the gaming rooms. John's outgoing nature quickly made him a favorite among the guests at the Raleigh. Many called him Johnny, and others, Jack, and some even asked for his advice on their bets.

"What do you think, Johnny? Should I bet on or against Colonel Washington?" Mr. Digges of Yorktown asked one evening when Colonel Byrd announced that he was taking bets on whether Washington could break open a walnut with his fingers.

Much to the delight of the room, John declared, "It is never wise to bet against Colonel Washington."

Mr. Digges followed John's advice and won his bet. Although such advice was always sought in jest, it made

John feel important and it pleased him that so many gentlemen asked for his opinion.

James was far less comfortable in such situations and usually stood off to the side, wishing not to be seen but ready to help anyone who needed his assistance. While he stood near these great men, James listened. Much of what he heard was gossip, but sometimes the men discussed politics and current affairs. Some even uttered shocking criticisms of the King and Parliament.

Patrick Henry was one who frequently expressed such criticism about England's leaders. James, like some of the older burgesses who visited the Raleigh, thought Mr. Henry was too confrontational with his endless criticism of the British Parliament.

John, however, thought Henry the greatest man in the colony. Although both boys were too young to remember Mr. Henry's Stamp Tax Resolves, they knew—by listening to the frequent recollection of them inside the Raleigh—that Parliament's passage of the Stamp Act back in 1765 was the cause of the ongoing dispute. And Mr. Henry's Resolves helped end the Stamp Act.

"No Taxation Without Representation," was the slogan they rallied around back then, and that sentiment remained strong in the colonies to the present.

"Gentlemen, if we submit to just one of their unconstitutional taxes," declared Mr. Henry one evening in the Apollo Room, "we and our children will become nothing but slaves to Parliament!" "

"Indeed, sir!" agreed Mr. Richard Henry Lee. "Parliament must understand that since we do not vote in their elections, they do not represent us, and therefore have no authority over us."

"Surely you do not mean *no* authority, sir," objected Mr. John Randolph, Virginia's Attorney General. "Parliament does have authority over the British empire and are we not part of that empire?"

"I concede Mr. Randolph," replied Mr. Lee, "that Parliament does have the right to manage our empire, and as we are part of the empire, that means they can regulate our trade with other countries, but you and I both know that the Stamp Tax and Townshend Duties were not meant to manage the empire—they were meant to tax the colonies directly. If we let them get away with that, there will be no stopping them in the future."

"Very true, very true, sir," agreed Mr. Henry. "All they need is for us to accept just one of their illegal taxes and then they'll use it as an excuse for another and another! And they won't stop with taxes," Mr. Henry paused for dramatic effect, "they will next argue that since they have authority to tax us, they also have authority to pass *any* law they wish over us. And since we do not vote in their elections, we'll be powerless to stop them."

"And hence will be nothing but slaves to them," added Mr. Lee.

Across the street in her father's tavern, Rebecca overheard a similar discussion. Colonel Washington and Mr. George Fairfax were dining together in the private club room, and by the sound of it, were not having a very pleasant conversation. She told James and John about it the next morning.

"I stopped in the doorway because Colonel Washington and Mr. Fairfax seemed to be arguing with each other," she said. "I couldn't hear everything, but Colonel Washington did pound the table and say, 'By God, Sir! Parliament has as much right to stick its hand into my pocket as I do to reach into yours, and if we allow them to do so, we shall be nothing but slaves to them!'"

The boys both smiled at each other.

"We heard the same thoughts last night from Mr. Henry," said John.

"I think they are worried that Parliament will try another way to tax us," said James.

Rebecca bit her bottom lip. "It bothers me to see Colonel Washington so angry about it. I've never seen him angry before."

The House of Burgesses finally adjourned in April and although business in the taverns slowed, there were still court sessions to draw folks to Williamsburg.

Rebecca turned eight in May and her father asked her to join him on his bi-weekly visit to the Market House to purchase fresh food for the tavern. She happily agreed.

The market was held every Tuesday and Friday across from the county courthouse. Vendors offered fresh beef, pork, lamb, poultry, fish, shellfish, and whatever vegetables were in season. Sally, the Anderson's enslaved cook, and her two daughters joined Mr. Anderson at market twice a week. She had done so for years and usually arrived an hour before he did to inspect the items for sale with her experienced eye. Her daughters pushed a small empty cart from the tavern that they used to transport all the meat and produce Mr. Anderson bought at the market.

Sally made all the selections for purchase, however.

When Mr. Anderson and Sally had first begun these shopping trips, Mr. Anderson would sometimes forget himself and buy items without Sally's inspection and approval—which always led to him paying a higher than necessary price.

At the time, Sally said nothing to signal her disapproval. But vendors soon learned that one sale behind Sally's back cost them at least two months of future sales. Because Sally *always* found a reason not to purchase from the wayward vendor until she felt he had been adequately punished for overcharging Mr. Anderson.

Sally never offered advice to Mr. Anderson in words—it always came in a look. Mr. Anderson would look at an item and then at Sally. A smile meant she thought the quality and price of whatever was being considered was fair. A blank or expressionless look meant no, something was wrong with the item or price.

When Mr. Anderson received one of these looks he would often turn to the vendor and ask for a lower price. If Sally smiled at the offer, or at the vendor's counteroffer, a sale was made. If not, they moved on to the next vendor. It was common practice for vendors to negotiate with Mr. Anderson, but sneak glances at Sally to gauge their standing and adjust their offer.

Rebecca did not realize what was happening in these transactions at first. She just thought her father was being very careful and shrewd in his purchases. But she eventually noticed the connection between her father's decisions and Sally's expressions and realized that it was *Sally* who actually made all the purchasing decisions each visit to the market.

Once shopping at the market was complete, Sally and her girls returned to the tavern with the cart. Rebecca and her father sometimes followed, but more often they continued walking and shopping, sometimes in Mr. Greenhow's store, sometimes in Mr. Prentis's. Her father always purchased something for Rebecca—a ribbon for her hat, a new fan or colorful neck scarf, or something sweet to eat. He had accounts at both stores and charged whatever he bought to them.

Rebecca adored her bi-weekly visits to the market. Not only was it an opportunity to see more of the city, but it was a chance to spend some precious uninterrupted time with her father. Mr. Anderson was a busy man and Rebecca saw little of him privately at the tavern. She missed the time they used to spend together at their old tavern. It was smaller and a lot less demanding of his time than the new tavern was. These walks to the market twice a week provided Rebecca an opportunity to be with her father again, and she thoroughly enjoyed it.

"How are you doing with your reading and sums?" her father asked as they walked arm in arm to the market. "Your writing is quite fine. I may have you write my letters soon. I'm sure those who receive them would prefer your handwriting to mine."

"Your handwriting is perfectly fine, Father," Rebecca laughed. "Besides, what would people think if they received a letter written in my hand but in your voice?"

"They would think, 'Thank goodness, Mr. Anderson has wisely hired his daughter as his secretary. I can finally read his letters,' that's what they'd think."

They both laughed at the thought of it.

Summers in Virginia sometimes arrived in May but more typically in June. It was just so in 1772. High temperatures and humidity that thickened the air with moisture settled upon Williamsburg in mid-June and remained until September.

With business in the taverns at its slowest point of the year, James, John, and Rebecca found themselves with more time to spend together. One of their favorite meeting spots was behind Mr. Dixon and Mr. Hunter's print shop, where a small brook flowed. Shaded by tall trees, the water ran cool and clear and the children sat upon the bank. They cooled their bare feet and shared stories of what they heard or saw in the taverns. It was their own little oasis, and the kindly printers did not mind their frequent visits.

There was another brook near the jail that the children sometimes visited, but the odors produced by the poor souls held in the jail awaiting trial were sometimes too unpleasant to tolerate.

It was during one of their visits to their favorite brook, while gossiping about their neighbors and the few visitors who had ventured into town, that the boys first called Rebecca, "Becca." John did so first, asking her why she was so critical of Elizabeth Farrow, the eight-year-old niece of Mrs. Margaret Hunter, the milliner.

Elizabeth had arrived from London late in the spring and lived with her aunt, who owned a millinery shop that sold ladies accessories just three buildings from the Raleigh. The boys were infatuated with Elizabeth's dress and manners—she was from London after all—but Rebecca was not impressed.

"I think she is conceited!" Rebecca huffed. "She thinks she is better than us. Just listen how she talks about Virginia and the colonies. I don't know why you two like her so much, she barely knows you exist."

James came to Elizabeth's defense. "Well, she was born in London and things are different there."

"That's right, Becca," added John, "everything here is still new to her. She just needs more time to get used to us."

James nodded. "I imagine it is hard to move from a place like London to Williamsburg, Becca. Kind of like leaving here and going to live in the wilderness."

Rebecca rolled her eyes and sighed. Elizabeth Farrow was a snob, plain and simple. They'd see soon enough. In the meantime, she took note of the nickname the boys had given her. She liked it. Her parents called her Becky out of affection so she figured that her new nickname with the boys was also a gesture of affection from them.

That affection was confirmed a month later—at least from John—when he challenged two older boys to a fight in Rebecca's honor.

Rebecca had agreed to meet the boys at the brook but had been delayed by chores at home. When she was finally allowed to leave, she rushed down the street. But as she descended the sloping ground to the brook, she tripped over a tree root and took a nasty spill.

Two boys, Philip Carter and Samuel Scrivener, were walking along the back street and saw the whole thing. Instead of offering their assistance, they broke out into laughter.

"*That* was graceful," Philip taunted.

"What's the hurry, Miss Anderson? Have to use the privy?" snickered Samuel.

Rebecca glared at the two of them and was about to comment on their ungentlemanly behavior, but before she could utter a word, John was there, helping her to her feet. He gave her a quick look over, confirming that she was alright, before turning and marching toward Philip and Samuel.

"You apologize to Miss Anderson now!" he demanded, eyes flaming, a pointed finger inches from Philip's chest.

Although the boys were older and bigger than John, his aggressiveness spooked them. There was a wildness in his eyes they knew not to mess with. Philip grabbed Samuel's arm. "Come," he said loudly. "We must go now, or we'll be late." And they walked briskly away.

John was furious at them but did not pursue. Instead, he turned around and went back to Rebecca, whose palms were both scraped by the fall.

"Can I?" he asked, reaching to better examine them. There was a bit of blood, but nothing too serious. He gently patted the back of her hand. "We'll go soak them in the water. Then you'll feel better."

Rebecca was struck by John's behavior. Not only had he risen to her defense, but he continued to focus on her in a way she had never seen before.

"Thank you, John," she smiled. "Those boys were awful."

When James heard what happened he reacted with mixed emotions. He too was angry at the boys who mocked Rebecca, but what troubled him more was that he didn't think he would have reacted the same way. James did not want to admit it, but he was a bit jealous of John's boldness.

The hot summer of 1772 eventually gave way to fall, and yet, Williamsburg remained unusually quiet and slow. Governor Dunmore saw no need to call the House of Burgesses into session so it did not meet for the remainder of the year. The courts still met, however, and people continued to come to Williamsburg to conduct business, but the absence of the burgesses—and of the people they attracted to Williamsburg—was felt by all the tavernkeepers in the city.

Mrs. Southall and Mrs. Anderson took advantage of this extended slow period of business to catch their children up on their lessons. Mrs. Anderson only had Rebecca to teach, but there was a new baby on the way—much to the delight of Rebecca and her parents. So, Mrs. Anderson increased the time spent on Rebecca's lessons, knowing that once the baby arrived, she would be forced to cut back. Rebecca's dance lessons with Mr. Fearson also continued.

Mrs. Southall had James and John, plus three younger children to teach and care for. John pleaded with her not to continue the dance lessons.

"I don't see the use of them," he complained. "I'm never going to dance when I'm grown."

"Oh, yes you will," replied his mother. "If you want to find a fine wife, you'll have to dance."

John just rolled his eyes, knowing it was no use arguing with his mother when she had her mind set on something.

Although the Christmas season did not formally begin until Christmas Day, James, John, and Rebecca felt the excitement of it several weeks before. James turned ten on December 3rd, and John turned nine on December 29th. In between their birthdays, a private ball was held in the Apollo Room.

James and John wore their best outfits—not to participate in the ball, but to work it. Rebecca did not attend, but Elizabeth Farrow and her aunt did. The boys tried all night to talk with Elizabeth, but she ignored them—preferring to spend her time with several of Mr. Nicholas's children. He was Virginia's treasurer, and his family was part of the wealthy gentry class.

By the end of the evening, James and John finally saw what Rebecca had seen in Elizabeth Farrow. She was indeed a snob who wanted nothing to do with the sons of tavernkeepers or any tradesman. As a young lady from London, such people were apparently beneath her. Even at just eight years old, Elizabeth preferred the company of the gentry class—or at least she *thought* she did. She would soon sadly learn, however, that despite her London background, those in the gentry class did not necessarily want to associate with her.

The Brook

Chapter 5

Fight 'Em!
1773

In early March of 1773, Governor Dunmore called the House of Burgesses into session to address the discovery of counterfeit paper money in the colony. On the eve of the session, a handful of burgesses—including Thomas Jefferson, Patrick Henry, Richard Henry Lee, and several others—met in a private room at the Raleigh Tavern. Rumors of new British policies for the colonies concerned them and they wanted to create a better way to communicate with the other colonies should it be necessary to oppose Parliament again.

James assumed his regular role as attendant, but was told by Mr. Henry to remain outside the door instead of inside the room. He could only hear bits of conversation between the men, but from what he heard, they wanted to create a committee of correspondence to write letters to the other colonies.

It takes a whole committee to write letters? thought James to himself. *They must be important.*

The letters were indeed important, designed to keep the other colonies updated on events in Virginia and to better organize a united response to whatever Parliament planned to do with the colonies. When James read the names of those on the Committee of Correspondence in the newspaper several weeks later, he recognized most of them. Speaker Randolph, Patrick Henry, Thomas Jefferson, Richard Henry Lee, Robert Carter Nicholas, and Edmund Pendleton were all influential Virginians who visited the Raleigh frequently.

"But how in God's name will Mr. Henry and Mr. Pendleton ever agree on what to write?" James asked Rebecca the next day, knowing how much those two men disagreed on politics.

"They will compromise, I am sure," replied Rebecca, "the way all civilized people do."

John listened to the discussion and rolled his eyes at her comment. *Sometimes one has to stand their ground on principle,* he thought.

Although the idea for a Committee of Correspondence was first discussed in the Raleigh Tavern, it was the House of Burgesses that officially created it on March 12th. It was the most important action the burgesses took in their short, two-week session. Mr. Southall was disappointed that the burgesses did not meet longer. He was even more disappointed when Governor Dunmore postponed another session, pushing it into the next year.

The Committee of Correspondence, however, met at the Raleigh Tavern on March 13th and again on April 6th. They wrote letters of introduction to leaders in other colonies encouraging them to form similar committees. Most did so quickly, and by the fall these committees had plenty to write about.

But the fall was still six months away. It was spring in Virginia, perhaps the most pleasant season of the year. Warm temperatures triggered an explosion of color across the landscape as the trees and wild plants bloomed and turned various shades of green.

Spring also meant planting season, and for a colony like Virginia, where nine out of ten families farmed for a living, that meant lots of tobacco—the cash crop—and corn—the staple crop—for the colony.

Although his main source of income was the Raleigh Tavern, Mr. Southall owned a 900-acre tract of land outside of Williamsburg upon which he grew tobacco, corn and much more. Five enslaved men, two enslaved women and an overseer tended tens of thousands of tobacco and corn plants every year. The tobacco was shipped to Britain in large barrels, called hogheads, that held over a thousand pounds of tobacco leaves per barrel. So, tobacco sales helped pad Mr. Southall's wallet quite a bit. They also allowed him to furnish the Raleigh with fine English goods and drink.

The Southhall's kept most of the corn for themselves, grinding much of it into corn meal for their guests, their slaves, and themselves. A portion of the corn was also used to feed their livestock. Cattle, sheep, hogs, chicken and a wide variety of vegetables were raised each year on the farm property and all were offered at Mr. Southall's table at some point at the Raleigh.

In May of 1773, Mr. Southall purchased another enslaved man to work his plantation and an enslaved woman for the tavern. He had rented Phyllis from her owner during the previous busy Christmas season and was so impressed with her work in the tavern that he bought her in May for £80. Mr. Southall was pleased with his shrewd purchase—Phyllis was a hard worker and worth more than the price he paid. He never considered how Phyllis felt about the change in her life or who she might have left behind.

Rebecca turned nine on May 3rd, and finally became a big sister three weeks later when her baby sister, Hope, was born. Rebecca was thrilled for her parents, but suspected her father was a little disappointed that he was not blessed with a son. If he was disappointed though, he never let on, and Rebecca embraced a whole new set of responsibilities and tasks to help raise her baby sister.

She continued to visit with the boys at the brook whenever she could, but such visits were far fewer than the previous summer. Little Hope and her mother needed her help.

Changes also occurred for James in September. He was enrolled in the grammar school at the college of William and Mary. The college, established eighty years earlier to teach boys Latin, Greek, Religion, Writing, Mathematics, and Natural Philosophy, was located on the western end of Duke of Gloucester Street inside an impressive three-story brick building. It was divided into a grammar school for young boys and a college for more advanced students.

James received the news of his enrollment with mixed emotions. He was thrilled at the opportunity to advance his knowledge, but terrified that he was not up to the standards of the school. Yes, it was true that he craved to read and learn as much as he could, but Latin? Greek? Natural Philosophy? His knowledge of these things was almost non-existent. Would he be capable of learning such things?

The school taught about 70 students a year. The grammar school students lived on the third floor of the college in a sort of barracks arrangement under the supervision and discipline of house ushers. Thomas Gwatkins, an avowed Tory who believed the actions of men like Patrick Henry and Thomas Jefferson were treasonous, was headmaster of the grammar school. James received most of his instruction from him.

Destined, however, to learn far more than Latin and Greek at the grammar school, James entered his new environment in the fall of 1773—one where privileged boys from prominent Virginia families ruled. Life for a tavernkeeper's son—even a popular tavernkeeper like Mr. Southall—promised to be difficult in such an environment, and it was just so for James.

All first-year students experienced some degree of hazing when they arrived at school simply for being new students. Whenever they encountered a student of the college, identified by the black robes they wore at school, first-year students were required to stop and bow to them and say, "Your servant, sir." Many of the daily chores of the student body fell to the first years and they were always the last to be served dinner. Such treatment was annoying to James and the other first-year students, but they could do nothing but accept it. It was part of the school's tradition, and tradition had to be upheld.

Within days of his attendance at the school, however, the treatment of James and several other students went from traditional hazing to outright harassment. It started with name calling. For James it was "tavern boy" or "bar keep." There were also frequent requests to empty chamber pots, make the beds, and bring pints of ale. Although such incidents bothered James, what hurt the most was how most of the students shunned and ridiculed him for being a son of a tavernkeeper. Most of his classmates were sons of wealthy planters and they looked down upon students like James. The "lower sort," as they called the sons of tradesmen and merchants, lacked the proper background, character, and education to be at the school and thus were an embarrassment.

James was miserable at school and wanted to quit. He was determined, however, not to disappoint his parents, so he did his best to ignore the bullies and focus on his studies. On visits home—which was less than a mile away straight down Duke of Gloucester Street—James insisted that everything was fine at school and that he enjoyed it. He did not want to worry or sadden his family. The small lie ate away at his conscience a bit, but he told himself it was okay because there was truth to his statement. He loved learning and *did* enjoy his lessons, rigorous as they were. But he wished the bullying would stop.

James turned 11 in early December and carried on at school until the term ended a few days before Christmas. He returned home for two weeks while the college was closed for the Christmas season and told convincing stories to his parents, siblings, and Rebecca about how wonderful school was.

Several days after Christmas, on the eve of John's 10th birthday, a grand ball was held at the Raleigh. James and John assumed their roles as assistants on call, watching the festive occasion in the Apollo Room from the corners.

James's cheeks burned a bit with shame when several of his fellow students entered the room with their parents. Here he was, a tavernkeeper's son, waiting to serve the sons of gentry. There was no clearer evidence that he was beneath them than this.

James wandered into another room to avoid the gaze of his peers and noticed some gentlemen gathered around a table engaged in serious conversation. He stood nearby and listened.

"Those damned hotheads in Boston have ruined everything!" one of them said. "They've gone and destroyed private property and made us all look like common hooligans! Yes, I agree the tea tax is still illegal and I oppose it, but dumping all that tea in Boston harbor was criminal!"

"Indeed," replied another, "they went too far! Nothing but mob rule up there."

A third gentleman speculated that Parliament would respond harshly to this "tea party." "I think they have reached their limit for such behavior and all of Boston will likely suffer for it."

James did not know what to think about the situation. Boston did seem to be a place where riots and disorder occurred on a regular basis. A Boston mob had looted and burned the governor's house nearly a decade earlier and another had provoked British troops into a deadly clash in 1770. Many called the latter incident the Boston Massacre, but others saw it as a riot that required British troops to restore order. And now there was a new incident in Boston. Something about a shipment of tea being dumped into the harbor. James did not know all the details, but he agreed with the gentlemen around the table—nothing good could come from this Boston Tea Party.

James shared what he had overheard with John and Rebecca the next day.

Rebecca shook her head. "Boston, Boston, Boston. Nothing good ever happens in that town."

John disagreed. "I like the way they stand up for themselves. I wish I were there."

James grimaced at John's words, thinking of his own situation at school. If he were more like his brother, willing to stand up for himself and confront his cruel peers, maybe the bullying would stop.

Rebecca noticed James's scowl. "What's wrong, James? Are you unwell?"

James hesitated. He wanted to tell her the truth, but he was ashamed.

Rebecca put a hand on his shoulder, her voice softer this time, almost a whisper. "What is it? What's troubling you?"

Before he could stop himself, James blurted out, "I don't belong at the college. I don't want to go back!"

Rebecca and John looked at each other, stunned.

"But I thought you liked it there," said John.

"I don't, I don't." His voice cracked a bit and he turned away. "It's awful. The others bully me for being a tavernkeeper's son and I can find no peace."

"Fight 'em!" shouted John, jumping up with his fists clenched ready to land a punch. "Put those prissy little gentlemen in their place! I'll help you and we'll whup the lot of them."

"That won't solve anything," Rebecca cut in. "Violence won't make you any friends."

"Friends?" scoffed John. "Why would you want to be friends with the likes of them? No, you must show them you won't be pushed around. A few hard punches ought to do it. And it'll feel good to get back at them for how they've treated you. I bet none of them have even been in a fight before."

Rebecca rolled her eyes. "Have *you*?"

"Well, not exactly," said John, looking at the ground, a bit hurt that Rebecca had apparently forgotten his willingness to fight the two boys who had insulted her honor. "But I'm not afraid to if I have to!"

Rebecca thought back to the day John had come to her rescue. It hadn't come to blows, but she didn't doubt it would have had Phillip and Samuel allowed it. John may be bigger now than he was then, but he was still quite scrawny—if Phillip and Samuel had been of a different mind that day, John might have taken quite a licking. Rebecca reached out to squeeze John's shoulder, her demeanor softer now, before she let her hand fall and turned her attention back to James.

"I think you should just ignore them. Don't give them any satisfaction by reacting to them. People like that know what they are doing. All they want is a reaction, so don't give it to them. Just focus on your studies and prove them wrong. Because you *are* as good as they are. Better, even."

James stared down at his feet to hide his eyes, which had welled up with tears. He didn't want John and Rebecca to see. He rubbed his chin in thought and nodded in apparent agreement with her, but inside he felt his situation was hopeless. Those boys would never change.

The College of William and Mary

Bruton Church

Chapter 6

I Appreciate Your Candor
1774

When James returned to school the following week, he was surprised to discover that he was wrong. His tormentors had seemingly softened. James was no longer a target of their abuse, but he could not figure out why. *Have they simply tired of the taunts or had the Christmas season filled them with kindness?* he wondered. But whatever the cause, he was grateful for the change. Sadly, it lasted just a brief time.

At the end of February, Williamsburg was abuzz with excitement. Governor Dunmore's wife and children—five of their six (the youngest remained in Scotland under the care of family there)—finally joined their father in Williamsburg.

It appeared to John and Rebecca that the entire city turned out along Duke of Gloucester Street to cheer and wave to the Governor and his family as they passed in two carriages. John and Rebecca stood on the stoop of Rebecca's tavern because it was higher than the Raleigh's porch and they could see over the heads of the people who lined the street. It had been a long time since the Governor's Palace had young children as residents and the new arrivals were greeted with hearty cheers and waves.

Lord Dunmore, his wife and their two youngest sons rode in the first carriage, which was closed. John and Rebecca, standing on their toes, could see Lady Dunmore and one of her sons through the open carriage window, but the governor and his other son sat on the opposite side, their faces obscured by the carriage roof.

The older children followed in an open carriage. There was George, who was called Lord Fincastle, because at 12 years old he was the eldest son. He sat facing forward and showed little emotion, almost as if he wished to be somewhere else. Sitting directly across from him sat his sister Augusta, age 13. She occasionally turned to the crowd and waved, but mostly sat rigidly upright facing her brother. Next to Lord Fincastle was the Governor's oldest child, Catherine, age 14. John and Rebecca could not see her clearly because her brother partially blocked their view, but from the brief glimpses they caught, each believed Lord Dunmore's oldest child was very pretty. A governess sat in the carriage with the children, but John and Rebecca paid her little notice.

Williamsburg's leaders hosted a reception for the family in the Capitol a week after they arrived and Governor Dunmore held his own reception—a ball at the palace—a week later. Only the highest of Virginia's gentry class were invited.

Two weeks after their arrival, Governor Dunmore enrolled his two sons, George—Lord Fincastle—and William, into the grammar school. They did not board at the school as James and most of the other students did, but arrived each morning by carriage for their lessons.

The faculty and student body all turned out to greet the two new students on their first day. Their carriage stopped on the side of the building and Governor Dunmore exited first, followed by his sons. James heard the Governor say to James Horrocks, the President of the college, "May I present to you my son, Lord Fincastle, and his brother William." President Horrocks bowed solemnly but the two boys barely replied in kind. James's stomach dropped. If the governor's sons believed themselves above the President of the college, what chance did *he* stand?

The small party entered the college and James thankfully saw no more of the celebrity students that day.

He deliberately avoided them—knowing what was likely to occur if he did run into them.

Two days later, however, while walking across the front lawn of the college, James heard a voice behind him say, "Is that him? Is that the tavernkeeper's son?"

James turned around and saw Lord Fincastle, accompanied by a half dozen other students, glaring disdainfully at him. "Well, I don't think much of a school that allows *that* sort to attend," sneered Lord Fincastle. The boys with him snickered. "Come, let us away from such common stock." They all turned and walked away.

The knot in James's stomach tightened. He had been right, and he knew what lay ahead. Lord Fincastle, the Governor's eldest son, had just marked James as a target, and the bullying that had briefly stopped would resume—surely worse than before.

Fortune, however, shined on James. For the day after Lord Fincastle confronted him, Mr. George Wythe attended an evening of entertainment at the Raleigh.

Mr. Wythe was universally regarded as a brilliant lawyer and James and John admired him greatly. His constant quest for knowledge, keen legal intellect, and generous spirit, made him a fascinating man to be with.

James had seen Mr. Wythe many times at the Raleigh, always engaged in serious conversation about politics, law, and natural philosophy. He had never dared converse with him, but Mr. Wythe always made a point to greet James and John whenever he visited the tavern.

"Hello, young sir," Mr. Wythe said to John as he entered the Apollo Room. "How does your brother fare at school?"

Never one to hold his tongue, John replied candidly. "I'm afraid, sir, that it goes hard with James. Some of the boys treat him badly."

Mr. Wythe nodded gravely, pausing slightly before clearing his throat and continuing. "These things typically work themselves out in the end. I am sure he will be fine." He patted John on the shoulder and took a seat for a game of cards with several other guests.

The next day James received a stunning request, delivered by one of Mr. Wythe's slaves. He was invited to join Mr. and Mrs. Wythe for dinner. James was dumbfounded—he barely knew Mr. Wythe and had never met his wife. "This must be a prank," he thought to himself as he rushed to catch the messenger and confront him.

"No, sir," insisted the startled young messenger. "Mr. Wythe himself sent me with that message and told me to come right back."

"I see. Very well then," replied James, still thoroughly confused, but satisfied that the invitation was sincere.

As James made his way down Duke of Gloucester Street the next afternoon to Mr. Wythe's home on Palace Green, he noticed another student walking ahead of him, dressed as James was in his best suit of clothes. Behind James walked another such student, and yet another a dozen paces behind him. The boy in front of James turned the corner at Bruton Church and when James did so too, he saw the boy standing in front of Mr. Wythe's two-story brick home.

James approached the boy and nodded. "Good day," he said. The boy smiled meekly and replied in kind, looking at the ground uncomfortably. They were joined a few moments later by a third and then a fourth student and it dawned on James that they all had something in common. Everyone standing awkwardly in front of Mr. Wythe's house was a first-year student—and each was regularly teased and taunted at school by other students.

When it was clear none of the others would make the first move, James took the lead. "Well, shall we?" he said, sweeping his arm toward the front door as he spoke. He led the group up the steps and knocked on the door. Mr. Wythe's enslaved man, Ben—dressed in a fine suit of clothes—opened the door and welcomed the boys into the central passage. The walls were covered with the finest blue wallpaper James had ever seen. Images of ancient Greek and Roman ruins decorated the wallpaper and several chairs rested along one side of the passage. Mr. Wythe emerged from a back room and greeted the boys enthusiastically.

"Welcome, welcome, gentlemen. I am so pleased you accepted our invitation. Please, join me in the parlor. Mrs. Wythe is unavoidably detained."

The boys followed Mr. Wythe into the front parlor. A large red rug covered most of the floor, matching the red floral wallpaper that covered the walls. A large mirror and a dozen color prints of flowers, all framed, were spaced about the room on the walls. A coal fireplace provided warmth and a small harpsicord and music stand sat in one corner. Eight chairs were arranged along the walls and a gaming table with four chairs sat in the center of the room.

James went straight to one of the chairs along the wall and the others followed. None sat, however, because Mr. Wythe remained standing in the middle of the room, smiling.

"Please, gentlemen, rest yourselves," said Mr. Wythe, gesturing to the chairs. "I imagine you are all curious about why I asked you here."

Curious? James thought to himself, *I'm completely baffled.*

"Well," continued Mr. Wythe, "as you may or may not know, I have long taken great interest in the college and I make it a point to stay informed of what happens there. Mr. Gwatkins tells me each of you is a very promising student, so I thought I should like to meet you."

James was surprised. He was under the impression that Mr. Gwatkins thought him hopeless in mathematics

Mr. Wythe pressed on. "I thought you might find my collection of fossils and other natural artifacts interesting. And I was confident you would welcome a nice dinner for once—instead of another meal at school."

The boys all smiled at that, one exclaiming, "Yes indeed, sir. We most certainly do."

"Well then, let us get better acquainted," he paused, checking his pocket watch, "dinner is still a bit off." Mr. Wythe turned his attention to James first. "How good to see you, James. How fare your parents and siblings?"

"They are well, sir," replied James, surprised that Mr. Wythe remembered his name.

"And your studies at school? What subject do you enjoy best?"

James swallowed hard, a pressure rising in his chest. "They go well, sir," he stammered. "I think I enjoy Natural Philosophy the best."

That was not true, James enjoyed Latin and writing the best, but because Mr. Wythe had mentioned his collection of fossils a few seconds earlier, James thought it best to answer Natural Philosophy.

Mr. Wythe's interview continued with each of the boys. All said school was fine and agreed that Natural Philosophy was quite enjoyable. Just as the last boy, Thomas, finished giving his answer, Ben entered the parlor. "Dinner is served, sir."

Mr. Wythe nodded in reply and waved toward the door. "Gentlemen, shall we?"

James followed the procession across the hall into the dining room. At the far end of the table stood Mrs. Wythe, waiting with a smile for everyone to enter. The boys halted just inside the doorway and Mr. Wythe said, "Gentlemen, may I present my wife, Mrs. Wythe." She curtsied and the boys bowed solemnly.

Mrs. Wythe opened her arms in welcome. "Gentlemen, we are so pleased you have joined us. Please, be seated!"

The Wythe's dining room was covered with green wallpaper, adorned with several framed drawings of landscapes and another large mirror. A large map of the colonies hung over a coal fireplace, and most of the floor was covered by a green and white checked floor cloth made of heavy canvas. Mr. and Mrs. Wythe sat on opposite ends of the large square dining table and two chairs were placed on each side for the boys.

Upon the table sat a plate of ham surrounded by stewed onions, another of roast pork, and a third of beef lying upon a bed of green peas. Cauliflower, cabbage, and roasted potatoes sat in three other dishes. James and the others took their seats, picked up their empty plates, and began passing them around in a circle. Each person took a portion of whatever dish was nearest to them until every plate was full and returned to its starting place. Two young enslaved girls, just a few years older than the boys and smartly dressed, stood along the wall, ready to assist and refill wine, cider, and water glasses when needed.

Sensing the nervousness of their guests, Mr. and Mrs. Wythe worked hard to make conversation. James appreciated their effort and overcame his natural shyness to engage with them as much as he could. They talked more about school, then the upcoming spring, and finally, Lord Dunmore's family—an uncomfortable topic to the boys at the table.

"Have you met Lord Fincastle yet?" asked Mr. Wythe.

All four boys looked down at their plates, hesitant to answer.

Peter, who was a year older than James, finally replied. "He and his brother do not board at the college, sir. So, we have not had the opportunity yet."

Nathanael, the quietest of the four, added, "We did see the Governor and his sons arrive for their first day, but only from a distance."

James remembered that day and wanted to mention Lord Fincastle's rude behavior toward President Horracks, but he held his tongue.

When everyone had completed the first course, Mr. Wythe gestured to the enslaved girls and they cleared the table. They returned with a second course of lighter fare. A plate of roast rabbit, another of chicken, a large salad of greens with sliced radishes and boiled eggs, as well as carrot puffs and sweet bread were all placed upon the table. Seeing the sweet bread, James thought of John and chuckled to himself. Like his brother, James had no taste for it and declined when his plate reached the person serving it.

A third and final course of sweet meats—candied nuts, figs and ginger coated in a simple sugar syrup—chocolate biscuits, and strawberry tarts were offered to the boys after the second course was cleared away. The boys eagerly accepted and scarfed the treats down.

After dinner, Mr. Wythe brought the boys to his study to see his collection of fossils, coral, and animal bones laid out upon a table. This room was not as well decorated as the others because it was Mr. Wythe's private study—not meant to be seen by most visitors. The boys examined his collection and marveled at his optical viewer, which magnified whatever was placed under it. Even more impressive was Mr. Wythe's solar microscope, used to project an image placed on a slide upon a wall. As the boys admired Mr. Wythe's collection of artifacts and instruments, they relaxed and chatted with each other and with Mr. Wythe about each item.

Once they had completed their inspection of everything on the table, and admired the large collection of books and drawings, Mr. Wythe escorted the boys back to the parlor and joined Mrs. Wythe by the fire. He urged them to sit together at the gaming table, which they did.

An uneasy silence settled around the table. Mr. Wythe gave an encouraging smile, trying to give the boys a chance to initiate conversation. But when it became clear none would be the first to speak up, he leaned forward and cleared his throat. "So," he started, "what was your favorite item in my collection?"

James and Thomas agreed that the optical viewer was the most impressive. "The detail the viewer allows one to see on maps and objects is amazing," said James.

"The viewer is indeed fine," added Peter, "but the solar microscope impressed me the most. To be able to see the hair on the leg of a flea is unbelievable."

Nathanael nodded aggressively in agreement.

Another stifling pause ensued until James asked, "What do you think Parliament will do about the tea in Boston, sir?"

Mr. Wythe waved the topic away. "We needn't worry about that. I'm sure it will all work out." He checked his pocket watch and rose to his feet. "Well, gentlemen, I see the day is fading fast. We thank you all for your company, but I'm afraid you best return to school before it grows too dark. Can we expect you again for dinner next week?"

James and the others smiled broadly and said in unison, "yes, yes, of course!" They each thanked the Wythe's for their hospitality and left together, huddled the entire way back to school, chatting about Mr. Wythe, his collection of natural artifacts, and his very kind wife.

When he returned to the college, James reflected on the day. It was too early to say he had three new friends, but he had certainly met three comrades who knew all too well what he was going through at school, and likely sympathized with him the way he did with them.

On the afternoon of their next visit with the Wythe's, the boys walked together the entire way, speculating on what Mr. Wythe might show them from his fascinating collection of natural wonders. Along the way they passed several of their most frequent tormentors. One called out, "Where are you dregs off to?" But the boys acted as if they hadn't heard and walked on. Somehow the taunt didn't bother them as much as it used to.

On their third dinner with the Wythe's, the boys were surprised to find Mr. Jefferson in attendance. He had arrived in Williamsburg ahead of the next session of the House of Burgesses to oversee the printing of a pamphlet he had written entitled, *A Summary View of the Rights of British America*. It was inflammatory writing for a man whom James thought was even more reserved and shy than he was. James had seen Mr. Jefferson at the Raleigh on many occasions, and each time the tall, red-headed man seemed to disappear along the wall, much like James did, listening to the discussions that occurred. Rarely did he lead, or even join a conversation—at least at the Raleigh.

Despite his shy nature, Mr. Jefferson had a reputation as a brilliant thinker. He earned this reputation in part under the guidance of Mr. Wythe, who welcomed a young

Thomas Jefferson into his home a decade earlier to teach him law. Mr. Jefferson, however, had learned much more than law under Mr. Wythe's guidance—he had developed a great curiosity and thirst for knowledge of every kind.

After a few polite questions about school, Mr. Wythe swung the dinner conversation to politics and the Boston Tea Party.

"We should hear of Parliament's response to the Tea Party any day," began Mr. Wythe. "I must say, gentlemen, that as a lawyer I certainly cannot approve of the destruction of private property—no matter the cause—but I do worry that Parliament's response will be harsh."

Mr. Jefferson, who seemed much more comfortable at Mr. Wythe's table than he ever did at the Raleigh, agreed. "For the last ten years those ministers in London have misplayed their hand and I see no reason to expect anything different this time."

The boys listened intently, nodding frequently but saying little. Sparked by Mr. Jefferson's observation, Mr. Wythe, ever the tutor, asked the boys directly if they understood the nature of the dispute with Parliament.

"Well, sir," offered James, who had had the benefit of listening to gentlemen discuss and debate their long running dispute with Parliament at the Raleigh for several years, "it is my understanding that Parliament believes they have the right to rule over the colonies on all matters whatsoever."

Mr. Wythe, impressed by James's response, smiled. "Yes, yes, that is correct James, they declared it so eight years ago with the Declaratory Act. Do you know why that claim is so dangerous to us?"

"I believe, sir," James started carefully, "it is because we have no representation in Parliament. We do not vote in their elections."

"Precisely!" proclaimed Mr. Jefferson. "We have no way to hold the members of Parliament accountable. We cannot vote in their elections, so they need not *ever* consider what we want. Our views have no impact on them because we do not vote them to power."

"So, the Declaratory Act places us totally at the mercy of Parliament," said Mr. Wythe, "powerless to influence its members with our vote, yet subservient to their decisions."

"Just like slaves," observed James.

"Precisely," Mr. Wythe and Mr. Jefferson replied in unison.

Emboldened by the responses of these two extinguished gentlemen, James pressed forward. "But I have heard some say that we have an obligation to England for their help in the late war with the French and Indians. They also say we must contribute toward our share of the expense for the protection Great Britain provides us."

The other boys whipped their heads toward James, eyes wide. His statement seemed to challenge the views of the two great men before them.

But Mr. Wythe laughed. "Yes, I have heard that too. And in your father's very establishment—although not from his lips. Perhaps we do owe Britain a debt of gratitude. But even if we do, *how* we repay that debt should be left to us to decide—not Parliament. It is *our* elected representatives that have the power to tax us, not the English Parliament 3,000 miles away. That body has no right to dictate to the colonies on taxes, or any law for that matter, that does not involve the regulation of trade in the empire."

James nodded, but inside he was terrified that he had unintentionally offended his host and Mr. Jefferson. The conversation kept on, but James restrained his responses for the rest of the visit. As the boys prepared to return to school, Mr. Jefferson, much to the relief of James, took him aside and whispered, "I appreciate your candor tonight, Mr. Southall. It is important to consider all sides of the matter."

With daylight fading, Mr. Wythe and Mr. Jefferson accompanied the boys out the front door and down the steps. As they bowed and said goodbye, a carriage passed with Lord Fincastle and several of his fellow students inside. Lord Fincastle stared disdainfully at the party assembled in front of Mr. Wythe's house, but the other boys in the carriage were amazed to see the targets of so much of their abuse conversing with the esteemed Mr. Wythe and Mr. Jefferson.

James caught a glimpse of their reaction and felt a surge of satisfaction. Mr. Wythe smiled wryly at him and wished all the boys a good night. He had done the boys a great kindness with his dinner invitations and James was excited to see what the next day at school would bring.

The boys' association with Mr. Wythe and Mr. Jefferson had a magical effect upon how they were treated at school. The bullying came to an abrupt end. There was still an occasional dirty look and coldness from some of their classmates—especially those who associated most with Lord Fincastle—but the constant name calling and mocking ceased, and life at school became much more tolerable for James and his new friends.

The Wythe House

Chapter 7

We Cannot Remain Idle Spectators
1774

On the other end of town, John and Rebecca noticed an increase in business at their parents' taverns in April as some of the burgesses arrived in the capital early for the upcoming session of the House of Burgesses. The topic of Boston, the tea party and Parliament's expected response, was on everyone's mind.

John listened intently to the burgesses that gathered nightly at the Raleigh to discuss. He found Mr. Henry the most interesting. Henry predicted that Parliament would overreact and punish all of Boston—perhaps even all of Massachusetts.

"Those damn Ministers in Parliament have been waiting for an excuse to crush Boston," Mr. Henry declared, "and I think the Tea Party has given them that excuse. I'm glad they dumped the tea. It will provoke Parliament to reveal what they are really about—the subjugation of the colonies."

Some in the room thought Mr. Henry's views too extreme, but John agreed with him. *Mr. Henry is a man of frank talk and direct action*, he thought, both of which appealed greatly to him.

Rebecca heard much the same from Mr. Henry when he visited her father's tavern. His views did not appeal to her like they did John. She preferred those of Mr. Pendleton and Speaker Randolph, who both urged patience and held out hope that Parliament would be moderate in its response to the Tea Party.

They were not. Mr. Henry's prediction proved correct. Parliament passed a series of laws in the spring that severely punished all of Massachusetts for the Boston Tea Party.

The news arrived in Williamsburg in mid-May. Boston Harbor was to be closed, blockaded by British warships on June 1st. The city was to be occupied by thousands of British redcoats and the Massachusetts government was suspended, replaced by a military officer, General Thoms Gage, as acting Governor. In essence, Boston was to be strangled until those who destroyed the tea were identified and the tea paid for.

Upon this news, the tone of conversations in Williamsburg's taverns turned angry and militant. Even those who agreed that the vandals who dumped the tea should be punished thought that Parliament went too far in its response. Mr. Pendleton captured the view of many moderate burgesses when he declared in Anderson's tavern that,

> "Tho' it is granted that the Bostonians did wrong in destroying the tea, yet Parliament sending ships and troops to punish the entire city in a case of Private property is an attack upon the constitutional rights of all of Massachusetts. We cannot remain idle spectators to this."

Rebecca heard Mr. Pendleton's words and shared them with John the next day. He thought it grand that men such as Mr. Pendleton, who had always urged caution, now seemed ready to act. But Rebecca disagreed. All this confrontational talk with Parliament concerned her.

She would have likely approved of the meeting of a handful of burgesses in the council chamber of the Capitol that took place a few nights later. Patrick Henry, Thomas

Jefferson, Richard Henry Lee, and several others met to discuss how the House of Burgesses should respond to Parliament's harsh crackdown on Boston. They knew Governor Dunmore would likely dissolve the House and send the burgesses home if they reacted too strongly against Parliament, so they settled on a symbolic resolution that called for a day of prayer and fasting. The resolution called on Virginians to gather in church on June 1st—the date Boston Harbor was to be closed—to pray for Boston. It easily passed the House of Burgesses on May 26th, but when Governor Dunmore learned of it, he was furious.

"Those cursed burgesses have usurped royal authority," fumed Dunmore to one of his aides, "and I will not have it!"

Dunmore summoned the burgesses to the council chamber in the Capitol and announced that their resolution reflected poorly on them and worse, insulted the King. Therefore, he had no choice but to dissolve the House of Burgesses.

The members listened quietly, bowed when Dunmore finished, and left the Capitol. Many had expected this reaction and urged their fellow members to join them in the Apollo Room of the Raleigh to discuss how to respond.

John watched them stream into the tavern, some engaged in conversation, others silent, but all with determined looks on their faces. He was not surprised to see Mr. Henry and Mr. Jefferson enter, but when Speaker Randolph came up the steps, John knew this was to be a serious meeting.

Mr. Randolph led the meeting, attended by nearly all the dismissed burgesses, some ninety or so. Many had to stand because there were not enough chairs. Mr. Southall stood outside the closed door of the room, but John managed to tuck himself away in a corner inside the room so h could listen to what he knew was a very important meeting.

As usual, Mr. Henry dominated the discussion. "We must stand with Massachusetts in her time of need," he demanded. "Parliament cannot be allowed to get away with such an abuse of power!"

Others, like Mr. Pendleton, urged restraint. "It is best to proceed with prayer and fasting," he argued, "and hope our petitions and prayers lead to reconciliation with England."

The discussion dragged on and on, but the men drew no closer to reaching an agreement on what to do. So,

Speaker Randolph adjourned the meeting and urged the ex-burgesses to return the next morning.

The ex-burgesses gathered again in the Apollo Room the next morning and agreed that the day of prayer and fasting on June 1st should go forward. They also proclaimed that Parliament's excessive punishment of Boston was unconstitutional and intolerable and that Parliament's end goal was to establish its right to rule over all the colonies. The ex-burgesses adopted a statement in response that declared,

> "With much grief we find that our dutiful applications to Great Britain for the protection of our just, ancient, and constitutional rights, have not only been disregarded, but that a plan is pressed by Parliament to reduce all of the colonists in America into a state of slavery by subjecting them to the payment of taxes, imposed without the consent of the people or their representatives."

The statement went on to assert that Parliament's Intolerable Acts against Boston were, "a most dangerous attempt to destroy the constitutional liberty and rights of all North America."

In response to this, the gentlemen in the Raleigh pledged to boycott most British goods until Parliament ended its harsh punishment of Massachusetts. They also called for a general meeting of all the colonies to coordinate a united response to Parliament.

"An attack made on one of our sister colonies to compel submission to unconstitutional taxes is an attack made on all British America," proclaimed the ex-burgesses. "And unless the united wisdom of all be applied, the rights of all are threatened."

John watched from the corner as the gentlemen signed a Non-Importation Association, pledging them to boycott British goods. He understood the implications of this agreement. Virginia's leaders had chosen to stand with Massachusetts, and John agreed completely with their decision.

At least some of the other colonies did too, because the next day letters from the Committees of Correspondence of Pennsylvania, Delaware and Maryland arrived, each urging a united response to Parliament's actions. Delaware's committee went further and called for a

"Congress of Deputies" from each colony to meet and draft a single, unified response to Parliament.

Speaker Randolph, as the chairman of Virginia's Committee of Correspondence, read the letters and summoned the ex-burgesses to the Raleigh for another meeting. But many believed the Non-Importation Association of the previous day had completed their work and had left Williamsburg for their homes. Therefore, they did not receive Speaker Randolph's summons. In fact, less than half of the ex-burgesses attended, but they agreed with Speaker Randolph that a special convention was necessary to choose Virginia's deputies for the proposed Congress. Each county was instructed to elect two delegates for this convention which would meet in early August. Speaker Randolph then dismissed the meeting.

John stood in the Apollo Room after everyone left and marveled at what he had witnessed over the last three days. Virginia was throwing its lot in with Massachusetts. He was eager to share all the details with Rebecca and James, but Rebecca was busy at her father's tavern and James was still at school.

Two days passed before John saw them both at church. It seemed the entire city turned out on Wednesday June 1st to pray for the people of Boston. But when the three friends gathered outside the church after Reverend Thomas Price's sermon in support of Boston, it was not the exciting events of the past week that were first discussed, but the passage of another birthday for Rebecca—her 10th.

John had completely forgotten, but James remembered. "How do you feel in your tenth year of life, Becca?"

Rebecca smiled, happy that James remembered her birthday with all that had recently occurred in the city. John, on the other hand, flushed with embarrassment.

"Thank you for asking, James. With all the excitement, I had completely forgotten about my birthday," Rebecca replied, hoping to soothe John's discomfort a little. It was clear to her that he had forgotten.

John flashed her a small smile. "I hope your tenth year is the best ever," he said quietly.

"Thank you, John. It has been quite a week, hasn't it?"

Re-discovering his previous enthusiasm, John shook off the last remnants of his embarrassment and launched into everything he witnessed at the Raleigh.

"I never thought I'd see Mr. Pendleton and his friends agree with Mr. Henry, but right before my eyes they did," he said. "They wrote up an agreement to ban most British goods."

"Yes," said James. "It's called the Non-Importation Association. The gazettes printed the entire agreement."

"Yes, that's it, and they wrote it in *our* tavern!" John said proudly.

Like James, Rebecca was already aware of the Non-Importation Association. She let John go on about its creation in the Apollo Room though, because she enjoyed his excitement at seeing it drafted. She was also relieved that Virginia's leaders had chosen a non-violent way to oppose Parliament. The Non-Importation Association seemed a good compromise between those who were ready to fight the British in Boston, and those who wanted to stay out of Boston's troubles.

"This association sounds very reasonable," she said. "I think it just may work."

James nodded. "I hope so."

John wasn't so sure the association would work, but he kept that to himself. Before he could resume his account, Mr. Innes, the head usher at the college, called for all the students to gather and return to the school.

"Speaking of school," Rebecca said as she turned to James, "when does the term end?"

"In two weeks."

"Has this term been better than the last?" asked John.

James realized that he had not shared with Rebecca and John what had happened thanks to Mr. Wythe.

"Oh, things are much better now," James said, sparing them the details. "I've even had dinner with Mr. Wythe a few times."

Rebecca and John looked at each other in surprise. Dinner with Mr. Wythe—now *that* was impressive! They were about to ask James for more details when Mr. Innes repeated his call to the students. "Gentlemen, let us be off." James bowed to John and Rebecca, who replied with a bow and curtsey, and then departed. As they watched James leave, Rebecca was summoned to join her parents. They had shopping to do in Mr. Greenhow's store. She pouted her disapproval at having to leave before John could finish his story, but John shrugged his shoulders, trying to look nonchalant. "Next time," he told her.

Rebecca smiled. "Next time," she agreed before turning to join her parents.

In need of an audience, John sought out his parents. As they walked back to the Raleigh together, John told them the story of what he had witnessed in their Apollo Room—for the fourth time—still hardly able to contain his excitement.

Chapter 8

Betsy Farrow

A few days later, while Rebecca stood outside Bruton Church after the service waiting for her parents, Elizabeth Farrow came up to her and curtsied.

"Miss Anderson, may I walk with you?"

Rebecca was surprised by the request. Elizabeth had ignored her and the boys for two years and now she wanted to talk? What for?

Rebecca steeled herself, offering a gentle smile. "Why of course, Miss Farrow," she replied as she returned the curtsy.

Just then Rebecca's parents walked up. "Shall we go?" asked her father.

"I'm going to walk with Miss Farrow, Father."

Mr. Anderson glanced at Miss Farrow. She smiled back at him. "Very well," he said. "Lovely to see you, Miss Farrow," he called as he walked off arm and arm with Mrs. Anderson.

"'Tis a fine day, is it not?" began Elizabeth, her voice quivering slightly.

"Yes, indeed. I expect though that it will be intolerably hot by the afternoon."

Elizabeth bobbed her head a bit too enthusiastically. "Yes, yes, I expect so."

The two girls walked on in silence for half a minute or so until Elizabeth stopped and looked directly at Rebecca.

"Miss Anderson, I want to apologize for how I have treated you since I arrived here. My behavior toward you and others has been inexcusable and I am ashamed."

Rebecca blinked. Was this real? She agreed with Elizabeth's confession—her behavior had been inexcusable—but she never expected acknowledgment, let alone an apology.

But Elizabeth looked sincere. Her brow was creased with worry, her hands clamped tightly together as she waited for Rebecca's response. Rebecca sighed softly. "Miss Farrow," she started, patting Elizabeth on the arm, "there is no need to apologize. I confess that I did notice a coolness toward me, and others, when you first arrived. But I assumed that everyone in London was that way."

Elizabeth perked right up. "Oh, in a way, Miss Anderson, they are," she quipped. "London is a dreadful place. I am very happy to be here instead, truly. I'm... I'm just ashamed at how I behaved since my arrival."

Elizabeth paused to let Rebecca reply, but Rebecca did not know *how* to respond beyond what she had already said, so an awkward silence ensued and they resumed their walk.

Just when Rebecca thought the silence was becoming unbearable, Elizabeth took a deep breath. "Miss Anderson," she said. "I let pretense sway my conduct. I believed that being from London made me..." she bit her lower lip because what came next was difficult to say, "made me better than you and the others in town," she exhaled. "I acted that way because I wanted it to be so, I wanted to finally be accepted by the higher sort. So, I-I," she stared down at her feet, "tried my best to act like them."

Rebecca was speechless. What could she say to that? *Yes, you were a terrible snob, thank you for recognizing it?* Certainly not.

"I was a fool, Miss Anderson," Elizabeth continued. "It's clear that they will never accept a person like me into *their* society. And truthfully, after engaging with them, I am glad of it. They are not very..." she paused, careful of her word choice, "kind. But now I'm afraid that my horrible conduct has ruined any chance of being in *your* society."

Rebecca listened with mixed emotions. Part of her felt vindicated—the conceited Miss Farrow had fallen off her high perch. But another part of her felt sorry for Elizabeth. She came to Williamsburg as a stranger who wanted to be accepted by the best sort. Who wouldn't want that? Yes, her behavior was dreadful, but she clearly regretted it and was reaching out for help. Could Rebecca say she would have behaved any differently? She wasn't confident she could.

Rebecca reached for Elizabeth's hand and they stopped, turning to face each other. "I wouldn't worry about that, Miss Farrow," she said with a smile. "We're not picky at all about who is in our society. You should come with me to the brook tomorrow morning. John Southall will be there. He should like to meet you properly."

"Oh, I would like that very much," Elizabeth beamed. "Very much indeed."

"I shall come to your shop beforehand," Rebecca proposed, motioning toward it across the way.

"Yes, yes, please do," replied Elizabeth. "And thank you, Miss Anderson, for your kindness." She curtsied and turned to go into the Millinery shop.

Rebecca was surprised at how good she felt. For two years she had regarded Elizabeth Farrow as a snob, a little priss who would certainly never be friends with the likes of Rebecca—*and good riddance*, she had thought, *who needs friends like that anyway?* But now, seemingly in an instant, she was excited at the prospect of a blossoming friendship. It was more than that though—it just felt good to help someone in need.

When Rebecca and Elizabeth arrived at the brook the next morning, John was already there. His eyebrows arched as he took in Elizabeth's presence. Rebecca held back a chuckle. "Mr. Southall," she said, "allow me to introduce Miss Elizabeth Farrow,"

"It is a pleasure, sir," Elizabeth said with a curtsey.

John stood dazed for a moment before snapping out of it and returning her curtsy with a bow. "As for me, Miss Farrow," he replied.

John glanced at Rebecca, his eyes searching for an explanation, but she just grinned.

"I believe I owe you and your brother an apology for my awful behavior toward you in the past," said Elizabeth. "I truly regret it. I was not myself when I arrived here and it took far too long for me to realize that."

John again looked to Rebecca, but she remained silent. "I-I did not notice anything awful about your behavior," he sputtered. "I just thought that perhaps you were nervous and shy."

The girls laughed. "Who wouldn't be nervous moving across the ocean from London? It must have been quite hard to adjust," Rebecca said.

"Indeed, it was," replied Elizabeth. "But my poor conduct toward everyone only made it harder. So I hope you will forgive me."

John shot one last look to Rebecca, waiting for approval. She gave a small nod and John smiled. "Well," he said to Elizabeth, "if you insist. All is forgiven."

The two hours that Elizabeth spent at the brook with Rebecca and John were delightful, and she did not want her visit to end. Her aunt, however, needed her help in the shop in the afternoon, so when the bell at the capitol chimed twelve, she announced that she had to go.

By the time James returned from school—just two weeks later—Elizabeth had begun to apprentice as a milliner for her aunt. Her days were fully employed in the shop so she was only able to join the others at the brook on Sundays.

James was very impressed by the change in Elizabeth—who all three called Betsy by the end of the summer. He was also impressed by Rebecca, who had reached out to help Elizabeth when she was in need. *She really is a good person and friend,* he thought.

At the end of June, Governor Dunmore suddenly announced that he was heading to the frontier to command a militia force against the Shawnee Indians. Unrest and bloodshed had erupted there, and the governor was determined to secure the west for future settlement and profit. His absence from Williamsburg meant the convention planned for August could safely meet in Williamsburg without his interference.

This was good news for the tavernkeepers in Williamsburg—it meant lots of customers during the usually slow summer.

The first delegates arrived in the city at the end of July, and soon Mr. Anderson's tavern and the Raleigh were bursting with guests. James and John resumed their dual roles as attendants and observers, but the convention delegates who gathered nightly at the Raleigh spoke very little of politics in their presence. Such discussions were saved for behind closed doors or at the Convention. The talk around the dining and gaming tables of Williamsburg's taverns was thus about tobacco and corn prices, horses, and gaming.

The Virginia Convention selected seven delegates to attend the Continental Congress in Philadelphia in September. Speaker Randolph was joined by Colonel Washington, Mr. Henry, Mr. Pendleton, Mr. Richard Henry Lee, Mr. Benjamin Harrison, and Mr. Richard Bland. It was a distinguished group of Virginia's leaders, and the boys and Rebecca were familiar with each one.

Speaker Randolph departed for Philadelphia ten days after the Convention adjourned amidst great fanfare from the city's residents. James, John, Rebecca and Betsy gathered at the county courthouse with most of the city's residents to say farewell. The Speaker assured the gathering that he would do all in his power to represent Virginia's interests in Philadelphia. He thanked them for their well wishes, then stepped into a fine carriage and was off.

The end of summer brought a return to school for James, and the continuation of home lessons and tavern work for John and Rebecca.

The news from Philadelphia was sparse, while that from Boston disturbing. Several powerful British warships were anchored in Boston Harbor and several thousand British redcoats occupied the city. It sounded to some—John included—like an invasion.

In October, approximately fifty young men from Williamsburg formed an independent militia company to train once a week. John Dixon, the kindly printer as well as a city alderman, was selected by the volunteers to command the company and they mustered near the courthouse once a week to drill. John watched the company practice whenever he could—envious and disappointed that he was too young to join them.

The Continental Congress in Philadelphia finished its business by the end of October and their decisions were revealed to the public in the newspapers in mid-November. The Congress established a continental wide Non-Importation Association that boycotted nearly all British goods. A refusal to sell goods to Britain would follow in a year if Parliament maintained its harsh policies against Massachusetts.

Counties and towns in every colony were urged to create Committees of Observation to enforce the new boycott. Anyone caught violating the boycott would be identified in the newspapers as unfriendly to the cause of the colonists. They could then expect consequences from their neighbors.

The people of Williamsburg formed their committee on December 22nd, about three weeks after James's 12th birthday. Mr. Southall was one of 21 men, including Speaker Randolph, Treasurer Robert Carter Nicholas, and Mr. Wythe, to serve on the committee. James and John were very proud that their father, a tavernkeeper, served alongside such great men.

At about the same time the Williamsburg Committee was formed, and a week before John's 11th birthday, Governor Dunmore returned to the city from his successful western expedition against the Shawnee. Troops under his command had defeated a large party of Shawnee near the Ohio River in October and this defeat convinced their leaders to sign a peace treaty.

Many residents of the city expressed their gratitude to the governor upon his return. Captain Dixon and the independent militia company marched to the palace to honor the governor, but he sent a message that he was not available to see them.

In truth, Lord Dunmore was displeased to learn that such a militia company even existed. As governor, he was in command of Virginia's militia and he never authorized the formation of such a company, so its very existence threatened his authority. To make matters worse, it was not the only such independent militia company that formed in Virginia while he was away. Nearly ten such companies were created in various counties in 1774—a clear threat, thought Dunmore, to royal authority in Virginia.

Lord Dunmore briefly set aside his concern about the new militia companies in January, however, when his wife gave birth to another daughter. They named her Virginia, which pleased everyone, and Lord Dunmore held a ball in honor of his wife and daughter. For at least one evening in January 1775, politics became an afterthought.

Governor's Palace

Chapter 9

Are We Gonna Fight, Father?
1775

There were two topics that grabbed the attention of Virginians in the spring of 1775: Patrick Henry's call for "Liberty or Death" at the second Virginia Convention in Richmond, and William Pitman's conviction and death sentence for killing an enslaved child he owned.

As much as John admired Patrick Henry, he and Rebecca could not stop talking about the Pitman case. What fascinated John the most was that his own children testified against him. If they had not, Mr. Pitman likely would have never been charged. The law did not allow Black people to testify against whites so if Pitman's children had not told the truth, Mr. Pitman could have described the beating as an attempt to correct the dead boy's behavior. Instead, a jury heard from Mr. Pitman's own children that he beat the poor boy to death for no reason other than that he was in a drunken rage.

"I don't think I could do it," said John. "Testify against my own father."

"Even if he did what Mr. Pitman did?" Rebecca asked aghast. "He stomped that poor boy to death for no reason. He deserves to be punished for it."

"I know, I know. What he did was wrong. But to testify against your own father and help convict him—"

"He was convicted because he did wrong," Rebecca interrupted. "He *killed* that poor boy. You can't just kill innocent people."

"I agree, Becca, I really do, but to testify against your own father…."

Similar conversations occurred throughout Virginia in April of 1775, but they were soon pushed aside by other news.

Early in the morning on April 21st, well before dawn, twenty British sailors and marines from the H.M.S. *Magdalen*—which was anchored just four miles from Williamsburg in the James River—slipped into the city on a mission. Governor Dunmore had given them the keys to the gunpowder magazine, a large brick building near the center of town across from the county court house. Barrels of gunpowder, muskets, and other military items were stored there, and Dunmore wanted the gunpowder moved to the British warship to keep it from troublemakers like Patrick Henry.

The British sailors and marines loaded fifteen barrels of gunpowder onto a cart before they were spotted by a night watchman. Cries of "They're stealing the powder! They're stealing the powder!" spread through the city and a large crowd gathered at the magazine.

John was awakened by the commotion and followed his father to the magazine. Mr. Southall carried a fowler, a flintlock weapon used to hunt birds. Many other men brought their guns as well.

"Are we gonna fight, Father?" asked John as he hurried behind him. He did not mean to sound so excited at the prospect, but he couldn't help himself.

"I don't know son, I don't know," Mr. Southall said gravely.

When they reached the magazine, they found over a hundred people gathered with many more on the way. Most were men, many of them armed with a variety of weapons, but there were also a few women and children mixed in the crowd. The details of what happened to alarm the city were unclear. Several different stories spread amongst the crowd. Someone asked whether it might have been slaves who broke into the magazine, but he was shouted down by others who insisted it was British sailors and marines.

"What did they take? Where did they go?" many asked.

County Court House

Gunpowder Magazine

Speaker Randolph, who was preparing to return to Philadelphia to resume his role as President of the next Continental Congress, hurried to the county courthouse as fast as his large body would allow. It did not take him very long—it was just a hundred yards away. He climbed the steps of the courthouse and joined several gentlemen there. The growing crowd moved away from the magazine and toward the courthouse. Mr. Dixon, the recently elected Mayor of Williamsburg, shouted, "Gentlemen, gentlemen, order! We must remain calm. Mr. Speaker wishes to address you."

The respect the people of Williamsburg had for Speaker Randolph was enormous, so when they heard Mr. Dixon's appeal, they quieted down instantly.

Speaker Randolph stepped toward the crowd. "My friends, I know you are upset, but I assure you we will discover soon enough what is at hand here. Let us not be hasty. Let us remain calm and peaceful, you have my word that we will get to the bottom of this."

John watched with excitement and fascination as the scene played out. Many of the men around him were angry and appeared ready to fight. Someone shouted, "Dunmore is behind this, let us seize him!" A number of men murmured their agreement, but no one went any further. Their respect for Speaker Randolph was too great for anyone to defy him.

The men on the courthouse steps grew in number. Mr. Robert Carter Nicholas, treasurer of the colony, and Mr. John Randolph, the Attorney General, and brother of the speaker, had joined the crowd. They all huddled in front of the courthouse doors, most nodding in agreement. Mr. Dixon turned and announced that the city's Common Hall, a sort of city council, would meet inside the courthouse to draft an address to Governor Dunmore. He asked the crowd to remain calm and patient.

John waited outside with his father, wishing that James and Rebecca were there. This was an exciting and important event—he couldn't believe he was part of it! John saw Mr. Anderson in the crowd, but not his wife or Rebecca. The two of them had never left the tavern.

James, however, did arrive with a large group of boys from the school.

John noticed James in the crowd almost immediately. "James, James, over here!" he waved.

James shuffled his way through the mass of bodies toward his brother. John thought James looked much less excited than the others—in fact, he looked worried.

"What's happened?" James asked, his eyes darting around frantically as he took in the scene.

"From what I can tell, sailors from a warship in the river broke into the magazine and stole the powder."

"What? Why would they do that? They must have their own gunpowder on the ship."

"Isn't it obvious? They mean to disarm us so we can't fight back when they attack. It's just as Mr. Henry says, they mean to subjugate us. Everyone is upset, James, and many blame the governor." John lowered his voice to a whisper. "Some even want to seize him."

James's mouth fell open in shock. "My god."

Just then, the courthouse doors opened and the Common Council—led by Speaker Randolph—stepped out. Mr. Dixon announced that a delegation would go to the palace to speak to the Governor. He asked that everyone remain at the courthouse until the delegation returned, then walked down the steps with Speaker Randolph and several others, and headed to the Governor's Palace, less than three hundred yards away.

John wanted to follow, but his father extinguished that hope quickly. "We will do as we are told and stay here," he said to both of his boys.

Governor Dunmore had heard the angry crowd near the magazine and waited anxiously in the palace. If an armed mob approached, there was little he could do to stop it. So, he was relieved to see from his bedroom window not an angry mob, but a small delegation approaching his residence. Lord Dunmore let them into the palace, meeting them in the entrance.

'Mr. Speaker," said the Governor, "I am alarmed at reports that a mob intends to march upon my residence. Is there any truth to this?"

"Your excellency," replied the Speaker, "it is true that many inhabitants have peacefully gathered before the courthouse, but this is because the powder magazine has been breached and gunpowder stolen from it. Do you have any knowledge of this, sir?"

Governor Dunmore glared at Speaker Randolph, offended at the insinuation in his question. There was a long pause before he replied. "Well, sir, as you know, the security of the public's military stores rests with me. And having heard talk recently of a possible slave rebellion, I feared the magazine too insecure, so I sent the gunpowder to the *Magdalen* anchored in the river."

"Why, sir," asked Mr. Dixon, "did you have it removed under cover of darkness? Why not do it in daylight?"

Dunmore shifted uncomfortably. "If you must know, it was to prevent any undo agitation among the people. You can plainly see now why I was concerned about that." Dunmore waved his arm toward the front door, referring to the large, armed crowd waiting at the courthouse.

The delegation asked Governor Dunmore to reconsider and return the powder, but he refused. Concerned, however, that the crowd might still march upon him, he assured the delegation that he would deliver the powder within a half hour of any proper request for it from Williamsburg's leaders. "If there is a need for the powder," he said, "you shall have it."

The delegation warned Dunmore that the people would be unsatisfied with that response, but Dunmore stood his ground. "Well, gentlemen, so be it then." There was an awkward silence afterwards, which Dunmore himself finally broke. "Gentlemen, good day to you," he said as he bowed and gestured dismissively toward the door.

When Speaker Randolph addressed the crowd at the courthouse, they expressed anger at Dunmore's response—as predicted. Some shouted, "Let us go, we should seize him!" but the Speaker urged everyone to remain calm.

"Return to your homes," he implored. "Take no drastic action. Violence will not resolve this!"

After a long pause, several in the crowd shouted, "We should trust Speaker Randolph," and murmurs of agreement ensued. Some spoke out in opposition, but most turned to go home.

To the disappointment of John and approval of James, Mr. Southall was one who started home. He bid James to, "keep up your studies, son," and then turned to John. "Come, let us go."

Rebecca met John by the brook in the afternoon and he told her everything that occurred.

"Thank goodness for Mr. Randolph," she said.

"I don't know, Becca," responded John. "I think we should have marched to the palace and forced the governor to return the powder."

Rebecca shook her head. *That boy… always so quick to fight,* she thought.

For several days after the gunpowder incident, Williamsburg remained calm. Lord Dunmore sparked some concern when he was heard threatening to arm slaves and burn down the city if he or any royal official under him were threatened, but nothing came of his rash threats and most people dismissed it.

On April 29th, however, the peace of Williamsburg was shattered by the arrival of news from Massachusetts. British troops had marched into the Massachusetts countryside and fought militia. Virginians would learn in the days following that hundreds on each side were wounded and killed.

Although such news was awful to hear, what was just as troubling to Virginians was *why* the British troops marched out of Boston in the first place. They had sought to seize weapons and gunpowder in Concord—just two days before the gunpowder in Williamsburg was seized.

"That is *no* coincidence!" exclaimed John when he heard the news. Others agreed. It now looked as if there was an organized plot by British officials to disarm the colonists. Without gunpowder or weapons, the colonists would be powerless to resist if the British tried to subjugate them by force.

"There is only one reason they would do that," John said to Rebecca. "They plan to use the army to *force* us to submit to them!"

Mr. Henry had warned of this very thing—a month earlier in Richmond in his Liberty or Death speech. "We must fight," he'd declared then. The news from Lexington and Concord confirmed that the fight had already begun.

In early May, John overheard several gentlemen in the tavern say that Patrick Henry was marching to Williamsburg from his home in Hanover County with several hundred militia to demand that Lord Dunmore return the gunpowder stolen from the magazine. John thought to himself, *Well done, Mr. Henry, put Governor Dunmore in his place*!

The Governor made it known, however, that should Henry and his armed hooligans enter the city, he would fight them with a detachment of sailors and marines sent to him from the H.M.S. *Fowey*, anchored in the York River. He also placed several cannons in front of the palace. "I will see this city burned to ashes before those outlaws enter it!" he declared.

Once again, moderate leaders negotiated a compromise. Governor Dunmore agreed to pay over £300 for the seized gunpowder while Mr. Henry agreed to end his march and disperse his men outside of the city.

"He should have kept marching," lamented John. "I should have liked to see Lord Dunmore submit to *us* for once."

"I think it was best to compromise," said Rebecca. "After all, Lord Dunmore just might have burned down the city. Then where would we be?"

"At war," John quipped. "Then we could finally settle this thing."

Rebecca didn't respond. She just shook her head and thought, *War might settle things, but at what cost?*

Days after this crisis was averted, Lord Dunmore received a dispatch from London that included a reconciliation proposal to all the colonies. He summoned the House of Burgesses to meet in early June to consider the proposal.

Before they met, another incident occurred at the powder magazine that re-ignited outrage at Governor Dunmore. Several young men took it upon themselves to break into the magazine to obtain muskets. When they entered through a broken window, they were met with a blast of lead pellets from a spring-loaded gun set up by the governor in anticipation of such an attempt. One boy was seriously injured and another lost two fingers—but it was Dunmore who received the public's anger. They accused him of endangering the youths' lives with a monstrous contraption designed to kill indiscriminately. Some called for Dunmore's arrest, but others noted that the boys had done wrong themselves by breaking into the magazine. When it was clear the boys would recover, tempers cooled.

A second incident occurred a few days after the House of Burgesses met in early June. Lord Dunmore learned that Williamsburg's newspapers were about to publish copies of letters that he sent to British officials in London over the past winter. In the letters, Dunmore accused Virginians of disloyalty and rebellion, and recommended that the British government respond with force against them.

The governor realized that the publication of these letters—which were provided to the newspapers by members of Parliament who were friendly to the colonists' cause—would likely create another uproar against him, so he decided it was time to leave the city before that occurred. He and his family left the palace early in the morning of June 8th, and fled to the safety of the H.M.S. *Fowey* in the York River.

The inhabitants of Williamsburg were shocked at the news. Everyone claimed that the move was highly unnecessary, that no harm would *ever* come to the governor or his family. They seemed to have forgotten about the angry mob that had wanted to storm the palace six weeks earlier—or those who had wanted to arrest him a mere ten days ago.

As for the British reconciliation proposal, the burgesses ignored it. Parliament's offer was something all the colonies needed to agree on together through the Continental Congress, which continued to meet in Philadelphia.

James returned home from school a few days after Dunmore and his family fled. Once again, events over the spring had overshadowed Rebecca's birthday in early May, her 11th.

Since the bloodshed at Lexington and Concord on April 19th, Virginians had experienced their own gunpowder crisis, had their capital threatened with destruction, and witnessed the collapse of the royal government. The situation in Massachusetts was even worse. Thousands of New England militia were encamped outside of Boston, ready for another bloody clash with the British army. It occurred a few days after James returned from school, on high ground overlooking Boston.

The Battle of Bunker Hill was one of the bloodiest battles of the entire war—a clash that the British won, but at a very high cost with over 1,000 casualties. Just three days before this battle, the Continental Congress in Philadelphia had voted to take charge of the army in Massachusetts. They'd placed George Washington in command of the new Continental Army with the rank of General.

Their choice of Washington was calculated. The delegates in Philadelphia respected Washington's character, and knew he had experience at war, but it was his connection to Virginia that convinced the delegates from New England to support him. If one of Virginia's leaders commanded the new Continental Army, then Virginia—the largest of the thirteen colonies—would likely become more involved in the war to support General Washington, a fellow Virginian.

It was a brilliant political move, but an enormous challenge for General Washington. He was to go to

Massachusetts and take command of the army there as a total stranger to the troops. Washington worried in several private letters that he was not up to the task. But duty insisted that he accept the command, so he headed to Massachusetts.

James and John, like most Virginians, were very pleased with Washington's appointment.

"Colonel, I mean, General Washington, will take Boston before the summer ends," predicted John.

"I don't know about that," replied James. "But I do agree that he was an excellent choice."

Rebecca agreed that General Washington was a fine choice, but she worried for his safety. She still remembered his kind words to her when they met several years earlier, and she always enjoyed his visits to the tavern because he was such a gentleman to her. "I just pray that God looks out for General Washington and his men," she said. Then, in a softer voice, "Do you think we'll have a war here, too?"

John thought to himself, *I hope so,* but it was James who answered first. "I don't know, Becca. I hope not."

"I think we will," John insisted. "Lord Dunmore is not one who runs from a fight. I bet he's stewing on that ship ready to explode, just waiting for a chance to attack. But Mr. Henry will be ready for him, you can bet on that."

"I just can't imagine my father and yours fighting against British soldiers. We're all British!" Rebecca cried. "Why can't we settle this peacefully?"

"I'm afraid it's gone too far for that," said James sadly. "Parliament will want revenge for what happened in Massachusetts and we'll have to pick sides."

"But we already know what side we're on, don't we?" said John. "I mean, there's really only *one* side to this. Isn't there?"

"Not for everyone, John," answered James.

He was thinking of his friend William Wormley, one of the students at William and Mary that he had befriended. James and William were the same age, but of very different backgrounds. William was the son of Ralph Wormley of Middlesex County, a wealthy planter from a prominent Virginia family. During the previous term, the two boys developed a friendship that overcame their differences in family status and views on politics. While James leaned toward the moderate views of Speaker Randolph and Edmund Pendleton, William held the views of the Attorney General, John Randolph, who thought that

Virginians should stay out of the mess in Massachusetts and not be aggressive toward Parliament.

"I agree that Parliament is wrong to tax us," William insisted to James one night at school, "but boycotts and threats from Mr. Henry of 'liberty or death' do nothing to resolve the dispute. They only make Parliament more determined to punish us."

James shook his head. "But surely you see that our letters and petitions to Parliament and the King have failed. We must do something stronger to change their minds."

"Those troublemakers in Massachusetts have certainly done that," William scoffed. "Do you want British troops here too, James? Because that or something worse *will* happen if we listen to Mr. Henry and his crowd."

Of course, things had turned worse since the two friends had this discussion earlier in the spring. Bloodshed in Massachusetts, gunpowder stolen from the magazine, and Dunmore's flight from the capital were proof of that.

Reports at the end of June that British troops were sailing for Virginia alarmed everyone. Several hundred militia from outlying counties marched to Williamsburg in response, prepared to fight. They encamped in tents in Waller's Grove, on the east side of the Capitol, and many dined and spent much of their time each night in the taverns.

John was thrilled at their presence and visited the camp as often as he could. The troops were rather disorderly, lacking proper military skill or discipline, but they were in the city and ready to fight and John thought that was grand.

At least one of the officers encamped at Waller's Grove, however, worried about the disorder in camp and complained to his friend, Thomas Jefferson, that the officer in command of the troops—Captain Charles Scott—was afraid to discipline them.

"Captain Scott, who is a good man and officer, fears he'll offend the men with firm discipline," complained the officer to Mr. Jefferson. "As a result, there is much disorder in camp. We appear rather to feast than fight. Southall's and Anderson's taverns entertain us elegantly," he continued sarcastically.

James, John, and Rebecca helped serve the militia officers and men who visited their taverns every afternoon and evening.

"They seem pretty confident," observed Rebecca one day at the brook.

"Shouldn't they be?" replied John. "There are hundreds of them."

"But they don't appear much like soldiers," said James.

"In time they will," said John confidently.

Virginia's leaders shared James's concern and acted to address the problem in August. Another Convention, the third, met in Richmond and voted to raise two regiments of full-time soldiers—over 1,000 men—to serve for one year. It was expected that these troops, called regulars, would become as disciplined and well-trained as any British redcoat.

Williamsburg's leaders also acted to better defend their city. They formed two new militia companies from the residents of Williamsburg. As a respected leader in the city, James Southall was chosen to command one of the companies. John and James could not have been prouder, and John asked his father if he could serve as his aide. "I'm sorry son," replied Captain Southall, "eleven is too young for such duty."

John wanted to correct his father, *I'm eleven and a half*, he thought—but he knew it was hopeless to do so. His father's mind was made up.

Rebecca's father was also given command of troops that summer. Captain Anderson commanded a company of minutemen raised in Williamsburg and the surrounding area. The men who joined this unit were expected to train more than the regular militia and be prepared to serve at a moment's notice.

Mr. Anderson was proud of his appointment. It proved his fellow residents in Williamsburg respected him. Rebecca, however, was petrified that her father would get hurt. But she tried her best to keep those fears to herself—she did not want her unease to take away from his sense of accomplishment.

Edge of Waller's Grove

Chapter 10

Williamsburg Becomes an Armed Camp
1775

In late September, the first of the new full-time soldiers, known as regulars, arrived in Williamsburg. A camp was set up behind the college, but as more and more men arrived, it spread beyond—onto the college grounds and eventually into the city.

The fall term at the college had already been delayed by the departure of several faculty whose loyalty to Great Britain and support for Governor Dunmore prompted them to leave Williamsburg. The continued disruption caused by hundreds of troops about the college triggered the cancelation of the entire fall term.

With his formal schooling suspended, James remained at the Raleigh, which was busier than ever due to all the soldiers in town.

Williamsburg looked like a military post by mid-October, with nearly a thousand troops encamped at the college and near the powder magazine. Scores of officers went about town each day in search of clothing, weapons, gear, and food for their men. They managed to feed their men just fine, but shortages existed in all the other areas.

Many of the officers spent time in the taverns in the evenings. John listened intently as they speculated about which regiment they would be attached to—either Colonel Patrick Henry's 1st Virginia Regiment or Colonel William Woodford's 2nd Virginia Regiment.

John was pleased that Colonel Henry, as commander of the 1st Virginia Regiment, was the ranking officer in Virginia. *He's a natural leader. I bet his men will follow him anywhere*, he thought.

Many of Virginia's political leaders disagreed, however. They were troubled by Henry's lack of military experience and tried to appoint another person in his place. But Patrick Henry was too popular and wanted the command, so he was appointed colonel of the 1st Virginia Regiment by the third Virginia Convention.

Colonel Henry and Colonel Woodford focused their attention on discipline and drills for the troops. The regulars were meant to be the backbone of Virginia's defenses—but they had to be properly trained first.

Governor Dunmore had sailed to Norfolk in July. He was joined in August by 120 British redcoats from St.

Augustine, Florida. These few troops, and several British warships, were all that Dunmore had to challenge the rebels in Williamsburg. As a result, he was forced to limit his operations to the area around Norfolk.

With all the excitement and business in the taverns of Williamsburg that fall, it was difficult for John and Rebecca to continue their daily lessons. Their mothers were far too busy with tavern responsibilities and the care of their younger siblings. Tutors were always an option, but the demand for them skyrocketed once the college closed, and it was impossible to find one to hire. James tried to substitute for their mother and instruct John, but he was not very effective, as John was not the best listener. James had a much easier time teaching his younger siblings instead.

Dance lessons had ended in July when Mr. Fearson suddenly left Williamsburg. John believed he did so because he was a Tory who supported Lord Dunmore. His sudden flight pleased John, who had always despised dance lessons anyway, but Rebecca was disappointed. Dancing was a joy to her and she missed the lessons—no matter Mr. Fearson's political views.

In place of their lessons, the children took on more work in the taverns, which were busy constantly. All three assumed the role of hosts for their parents, who were often pulled in several directions at once by the steady stream of guests. The children still managed to visit with each other some mornings, and they occasionally found time to walk about town to see all the excitement, but much of their day and evening was devoted to serving the guests of their taverns.

On one of their rare morning walks, John talked the others into visiting the military camp behind the college. It was not what they expected.

Spread all over the back of the college were rows of cloth and wooden tents. Four men shared each tent, which offered some protection from the sun or rain, but little protection from the cold. The ground around the tents and the entire camp was wet and muddy from the constant coming and going of the troops, and there was an unpleasant smell that lingered in the air. It was the smell of unwashed men and necessaries (toilets). The smell was made worse by the tendency of many of the soldiers to relieve themselves wherever they pleased. It was easier to do so than walk all the way to the necessaries that had been dug further away from camp.

"Good Heavens," gasped Rebecca, holding a handkerchief to her nose. "I don't know how they can abide it."

James was also troubled by the smell, but John just shrugged. "It's no worse than the camp this summer in the grove. Army camps all smell like this I guess."

In truth, the camp of Virginia's regulars behind the College was much better organized and managed than the one the militia volunteers that had been created in Waller's Grove earlier that summer. The disorderly first impression visitors had of the camp was more the result of the constant arrival of new troops than the complete lack of discipline that plagued the summer volunteers.

It was true that there was still a lot of work to be done to properly train and discipline the new troops—their choice of bathroom spots was evidence of that—but Colonel Henry and the other officers in camp issued daily orders to address such problems, and those who disobeyed faced court martial and punishment.

John was thrilled to watch platoons and companies of men drill on the parade ground near the tents. And he was not alone. Scores of people came to camp to watch the troops drill. "They are getting better," John insisted on a second visit to camp.

"Yes, they certainly do march better than before," agreed James. "But I wish they all had real muskets instead of those wooden clubs."

Providing all the troops with proper weapons, namely, a musket or rifle, was an enormous challenge for Virginia's leaders. Many of the men brought their own weapons from home, usually a fowler or rifle, but just as many men did not have such weapons and there were not enough muskets in the public magazine to arm all the troops who needed one.

The principal weapon of European troops in the 18th century was a smoothbore flintlock musket. The English called their muskets the Brown Bess. It was the weapon the British army used and it was designed specifically for 18th century warfare. Its heavy wooden stock could handle the stress of army life and serve as a club to bash the enemy if necessary. The rapid firepower of the musket—which in a trained soldier's hand could fire four shots a minute—and the 18-inch bayonet attached to the musket in order to stab the enemy, made the Brown Bess a fearsome weapon.

Proper training and discipline were key, however, to winning a battle in the 18th century. The main goal of an army in battle was to drive the enemy from the field, to break their lines and scatter them. If this happened often enough, the enemy would likely give up and quit fighting.

To achieve victory with a weapon like the Brown Bess musket, which had an effective range of just 100 yards (the length of a football field) proper training and discipline were required. Platoons and companies of soldiers fired at the same time in volleys and fought in two ranks (lines) standing shoulder to shoulder, with the rear rank firing over the shoulder of the front rank.

The wall of lead musket balls fired in a volley could devastate the enemy, but it was the bayonet that often determined the outcome of battle. A wall of soldiers advancing at charged bayonets was a frightening sight— one that often caused those facing it to run away. It took training, discipline, and courage to stand firm against a bayonet charge—and it took those same qualities to carry one out.

The problem for the Virginians and their fellow American troops throughout the colonies was that they did not have nearly enough Brown Bess muskets for all their men. The fowlers and rifles that some brought to camp were better than nothing, but neither could mount a bayonet, and the civilian guns were damaged more easily that the sturdy Brown Bess muskets. But even worse than that was the fact that many of the men had no gun of any kind. They used wooden clubs in place of a real weapon to train with.

Those poor men won't have a chance against the redcoats, thought Rebecca to herself. *What a dreadful waste. War is so awful.*

John thought the troops looked just fine, with or without weapons, and wished he, at nearly 12 years old, could join them.

James was more in line with Rebecca and pitied the soldiers without muskets. *I'm sure they won't be sent into battle without muskets though*, he thought. *They'll find them somewhere.*

The lack of weapons was not the only shortage the Virginia troops faced. The supply of gunpowder and lead to make musket balls was alarmingly low. The children, of course, were not aware of this, but Colonel Henry certainly was and pleaded with Virginia's new Committee of Safety to provide more of each item. This committee had authority over the troops and the colony when the Virginia Convention was not in session. The Third Convention completed its business in late August and the fourth Convention was scheduled to meet in Williamsburg in December, so between those sessions, the Committee of Safety governed Virginia. They did all they could to supply the army, but despite their efforts, Colonel Henry complained that he could only supply each soldier with a handful of cartridges, instead of the twenty-four rounds a full cartridge box held.

At the end of October, news of a clash thirty miles away in Hampton reached Williamsburg. British ships had attempted to bombard and burn the town of Hampton, but Virginia troops fought them off from shore for two days and stopped them. The newspapers were full of accounts of the battle. One claimed that Captain George Nicholas, the son of Treasurer Robert Carter Nicholas, fired the first shot. Other accounts blamed the British.

"It doesn't matter who fired the first shot," John insisted to James and Rebecca. "What matters is that we stopped Dunmore and his pirates from burning Hampton!"

John was excited that a battle had *finally* occurred in Virginia—but James and Rebecca were concerned.

Although fighting in the colonies had started six months earlier at Lexington and Concord in Massachusetts, the war in New England was 700 miles away and no blood had been shed in Virginia. That is, until the fighting in Hampton.

Although Lord Dunmore—who was still aboard a British warship off Norfolk—had just 120 British redcoats with him, he sent them ashore in the fall to seize weapons and gunpowder whenever he learned of their hiding places. Despite the limited number of troops at his disposal, no one in Norfolk and Princess Anne County dared oppose him. Now that blood had been shed across the river in Hampton, however, fighting would likely spread to other locations.

The confidence in Williamsburg inspired by the successful defense of Hampton was shaken in early November by shocking news from Philadelphia. Peyton Randolph, President of the Continental Congress, Speaker of Virginia's House of Burgesses, and Williamsburg's most prominent resident, had died. A deep sadness swept over the city, but there was no time to dwell on their loss. Several armed vessels crewed by British sailors were spotted off James Island. Their main purpose was to prevent rebel troops from crossing the James River, but their presence alarmed the residents of Williamsburg. The ships fired cannons at Virginia troops on shore, who fired back with rifles. A house on James Island was damaged, but thankfully the British never tried to land troops ashore. Nevertheless, the inhabitants of Williamsburg listened to cannon and rifle fire on the river for several days and braced for a possible attack.

"I'm not worried," John said when he, James, and Rebecca gathered with others near the courthouse to listen to the gunfire. "There are plenty of troops here to protect us."

"But what about the poor men fighting?" asked Rebecca, thinking that one day soon it could be her father. "I'm worried about *them*."

"Don't worry, Becca," said James. "I'm sure the ships are just making a lot of noise. The newspapers say the Governor has few men and I'm sure they won't be foolish enough to try to land."

"But if they are," declared John, his fists clenched, "we'll slaughter them!"

Although it was indeed true that Lord Dunmore had less than two hundred redcoats and Tories under arms to fight for him, the 120 redcoats of the 14th British Regiment won an important victory in mid-November at Kemps Landing near Norfolk. Dunmore's men suffered no casualties, but several rebel militia were killed and wounded, several more were captured, and the rest fled in all directions. Dunmore followed this victory with a stunning proclamation that called on all Virginians to rally to the Kings standard (flag). He stated that it was the duty of every loyal Virginian to fight for the King. Anyone who refused to do so would be considered a rebel and an enemy of the King—even if they wished to stay neutral in the dispute. Harsh punishment was promised to those who did not support Dunmore and the King.

Dunmore's proclamation included one more item that shocked and outraged many Virginians. He offered freedom to any adult male slave of rebellious Virginians who joined him to fight.

Governor Dunmore had threatened to free slaves as far back as April—after the gunpowder incident at the magazine—but he had never acted on this threat until now. His offer of freedom applied only to enslaved men of rebellious Virginians, and they had to *fight* for Dunmore to receive their freedom. Although his offer of freedom did not extend to enslaved women and children, he hoped that many of them would run away too and cause such disruption to the rebels that they would be unable to fight against him. Dunmore cared not of what freedom meant to the enslaved people—he wanted only to cause trouble for the rebel colonists.

Word of Dunmore's proclamation spread quickly through Virginia and among the enslaved community. Within a week, hundreds of enslaved men fled to Dunmore. He armed as many as he could with muskets and formed them into a regiment commanded by British sergeants.

Some of them were posted in a fort near the village of Great Bridge to defend the main road from North Carolina to Norfolk. Others were put to work building an earthen wall around Norfolk to defend it from attack. Lord Dunmore planned to use Virginia's largest town, Norfolk, as his base of operation, and once he grew strong enough, he planned to return to Williamsburg and crush the rebels there.

James, John, and Rebecca felt the tension and concern rise in Williamsburg after Dunmore's proclamation. More than half of the people who lived in the town were enslaved—over one thousand men, women, and children.

All three of the children agreed that none of their slaves would ever run away to Governor Dunmore, but they suspected others in the city might.

One evening in early December, Rebecca was shocked to discover that she was wrong. She'd felt poorly all day and got up to use the chamber pot in the middle of the night when she heard a sudden noise in the courtyard behind the tavern and went to investigate. She was surprised to find Big John standing in front of her with a bundle of clothes in his hand.

She rubbed her eyes sleepily, confused at the sight before her. "John, is there something wrong?"

Big John stared at her with concern before he whispered back, "No Miss Rebecca, everything is fine."

But there was something in his voice that alarmed Rebecca. "What are you doing with that bundle?"

Big John looked to the ground and didn't reply. Rebecca suddenly realized what was happening and jolted awake. "Oh John," she whimpered. "You're not leaving us, are you?"

Big John grimaced at her words but continued to stare at the ground before finally lifting his eyes to meet hers. "Well, Miss Rebecca, I want my freedom, I truly do."

Rebecca couldn't believe it. "But John," she said, "has Father done you some wrong? Hasn't he always treated you well?"

"Yes, Miss Rebecca, he has, all of you have. But I want my freedom. I've wanted it for a long time."

Rebecca shook her head. "But you can't go. It's too dangerous. They'll catch you and hang you."

"Well, Miss Rebecca, they very well may, but I have to try. I want to be free," he said. "I *need* to be free."

"But they'll make you fight. You'll have to fight!" Rebecca's voice rose a bit, causing them both to fall silent as they listened to hear if anyone had stirred. When it was clear they had not, Rebecca continued, her voice barely a whisper. "You'll maybe even have to fight against Father."

Big John's frown deepened. "Miss Rebecca, I surely hope I don't have to do that. But I truly want my freedom."

Rebecca grew angry now. John wasn't listening to her. He was putting himself in danger, and she didn't understand why. Hands on her hips, she stood in front of him defiantly. "Now John, you just can't leave, I won't let you. Go back inside. I won't say a thing about this, I promise. We need you, John. You have to stay."

Big John stood frozen before Rebecca. Although she was the daughter of the man who possessed him, he was fond of her and her parents and wished them no harm. And yet his desire for freedom—something he'd wanted all his life—was too strong to resist.

He looked her directly in her eyes, his voice firm. "No, Miss Rebecca. I'm sorry. I want my freedom. I have to try."

Rebecca's shoulders slumped as she realized she could not talk John out of running. He was not going to change his mind, no matter what she said. But did he need to? Rebecca could still stop him. She could call out for help. But to do so would bring trouble for him, surely. The jail was already full with runaway slaves who had tried what Big John was about to try—run to join Lord Dunmore. She didn't want that to happen to John, or worse—for him to get hurt. But she didn't want him to leave either. For what felt like a very long time, Rebecca just stood there in front of Big John, hoping he would change his mind.

A few more uneasy moments passed before Rebecca gave a long sigh. "Well, John, you must be careful. There are patrols out looking for runaways. If you get caught, they may hang you. But if they don't, they will surely throw you in jail and probably send you away. So, you be real careful. Promise me."

Big John nodded, clutching his bundle of clothes tightly. "Thank you, Miss Rebecca, thank you. God Bless you, Miss Rebecca." Then he turned and disappeared into the night.

Rebecca stood alone feeling anxious for Big John, and then guilty because her silence was a betrayal of her father. The law said that John was her father's property, and yet she had let him run off. She could have stopped him, but she didn't. Not only would her family suffer from the loss of a valuable slave, but someday her father and Big John might meet on a battlefield and he might kill her father. The waves of guilt crashed over her relentlessly and for a moment Rebecca wondered if she should change her mind and wake her father. But she just couldn't do that to John—she knew what would happen to him if she did. So, with tears welling in her eyes, she returned to bed.

In the morning, she acted utterly surprised when Big John's absence was noticed. She swore to herself that she'd never tell anyone what happened—not even James and John. They wouldn't understand.

As Rebecca expected, her father was stunned when he learned of Big John's flight. But his shock soon turned to fury. "Damn him and damn Dunmore for putting the idea in his head," shouted Mr. Anderson. "If we get him back, I'll ship him off to the West Indies, the ungrateful wretch." He turned his attention to his daughter, his face still red with anger. "Rebecca," he growled, "we'll need your help more than ever now."

"Of course, Father, of course," was all Rebecca said.

Another convention, the fourth, was held in Williamsburg in December, and that meant more business for the already busy taverns in Williamsburg. Once again, the Raleigh and Anderson's tavern were overwhelmed with guests, and James, John, and Rebecca worked day and night to help their parents.

They learned from members of the Fourth Convention that an important battle at Great Bridge, ten miles south of Norfolk, had occurred on December 9th, and that Lord Dunmore's redcoats had been crushed in a foolish charge against the Virginians. John and James were excited and cheered by the news, but Rebecca worried about Big John. She doubted that he had reached Norfolk before the battle happened—much less been *in* it at Great Bridge—but it was possible that he was there, and she worried for him.

Lord Dunmore's defeat at the Battle of Great Bridge caused panic among his supporters and he was forced to abandon Norfolk. Dunmore, his handful of remaining redcoats and Tory Virginians, and hundreds of runaway slaves, once again took shelter upon an array of boats anchored off Norfolk. The situation had drastically changed after his loss at Great Bridge, and Lord Dunmore struggled to maintain enough support to stay in Virginia.

Meanwhile in Williamsburg, the fourth Virginia Convention decided that two regiments of regular troops were not enough, so they increased the number to nine. These new troops would serve for two years, a year longer than the original two regiments, and the Convention hoped that the Continental Congress would take charge and pay for them.

The events of the fall of 1775 had brought Virginia fully into the war and John was thrilled. He was confident that the colonies would smash Britain and finally settle the dispute with Parliament. James and Rebecca, however, were less confident and worried more about the death and destruction that they felt waited for both sides.

Chapter 11

Independence
1776

Shocking news reached Williamsburg late on New Years Day. Norfolk was ablaze! Rebecca heard it first from several members of the Committee of Safety who were dining at the tavern, and the boys learned of it soon after from members of the Convention who were staying at the Raleigh. Everyone was convinced that Lord Dunmore was at fault, and the truth was he *did* have soldiers set warehouses on fire along the shore to prevent Virginian troops from hiding in them. But the real source of the blaze that ravaged the entire city was the Virginians themselves.

Convinced that most of the residents of Norfolk were Tories who supported Dunmore, Virginian troops took advantage of the first fires set by Lord Dunmore and ignited many more throughout the town. Over 900 buildings were destroyed in the massive blaze that raged for days.

Virginians did not know the role their own troops played in the fire, however, and blamed Dunmore for it.

Many questioned why they should remain loyal to a government or people that allowed its officials to burn entire cities and towns at will. The whole purpose of government, argued the English philosopher John Locke a century earlier, was to *protect* the people. But it was the British government itself—in the form of its chief appointee, Lord Dunmore—who abused them by stealing their slaves and burning Norfolk to the ground.

After the news of the fire, James, John, and Rebecca heard talk of independence from Great Britain for the first time in the taverns. Hushed conversations among Convention delegates and others grew louder as people read installments of Thomas Paine's pamphlet, *Common Sense*, in the newspapers.

James, John, and Rebecca each read Mr. Paine's words and argued about their value.

"His ideas are too extreme," said James. "He wants to end the monarchy and create a republic, like the Romans. But there's a reason there have been so few republics in history. I agree with some of what he says about Parliament's wrongdoings, but his vision for the future is unrealistic."

John found Mr. Paine's writing exciting, a rarity for any writing for John. "Well, I think he hits the nail on the head," he said. "Parliament has mistreated us for too long and has no right to rule or regulate the colonies. Our time has come! Parliament has pushed us to the point that *independence* is the only solution."

Rebecca cleared her throat, drawing the boys' gaze to her. "I still think we can compromise with each other," she said. "We have too much history to just throw it all away. We're still English after all. My hope is that our friends in Parliament can convince the others that we will never submit to them, so the only solution is to seek a compromise with us.

"We *are* still English, I agree with you there, Becca," replied James. "But the problem is that Parliament seems to have forgotten that and has treated us like a foreign people for as long as I can remember."

"Indeed James, you are absolutely right, and they mean to conquer us, not compromise with us," added John, turning to Rebecca as he spoke.

Rebecca had no reply to that. She feared that what they said was true.

"And since they've had ten years to change their ways," continued John, "but refused to do so, it seems to me that Mr. Paine's argument for independence is the solution that makes the most sense."

"Perhaps it is," replied James. "But that is a mighty big step to take. And if we *did* separate from Britain, we'd be on our own to fend off the French and Spanish, and Lord knows who else."

"We wouldn't be completely alone," noted Rebecca. "The other colonies would join us, wouldn't they?"

"Of course they would," insisted John. "Massachusetts and their neighbors have sought independence for years. Just look at all the fighting they've done! You can't go back to normal after all that fighting. They've just been waiting for Virginia to lead the way."

"You're probably right," said James. "Those folks in New England were ripe for independence a long time ago. But I'm not so sure about the others. I heard Mr. Lee complaining about New York just the other day. He said they wouldn't even support the boycott. So, I doubt they'd support independence."

"Who needs New York anyway," John scoffed. "We'll do fine without them!"

"Perhaps, perhaps," said James. "But it would be better if *all* the colonies stayed united. I think Parliament will give us an even bigger fight if we try to become independent."

Rebecca was bothered by all this talk. Although the dispute with Parliament had lasted as long as she could remember, she wished the fighting would stop and the two sides could solve things peacefully. Deep down though, she knew it was too late for that. Still, she wished for it with all her heart.

The fourth Virginia Convention completed its business in Williamsburg in mid-January 1776 and the delegates returned to their homes. The college remained closed, and the first of the new troops the Convention called for arrived in Williamsburg in March. There were now nine regiments of regulars instead of two, and although most of the regiments were not stationed in Williamsburg, their officers traveled there to receive their commissions and one new regiment, the 6th Virginia, was ordered to muster in the capital.

The fighting at Great Bridge in December had drawn the 2nd Regiment and part of the 1st Regiment out of Williamsburg over the winter. The departure of the

Convention brought a degree of quiet in the city that its residents had not seen since the previous winter.

The sudden resignation of Colonel Patrick Henry from the army in late February in a dispute over rank replaced the calm that had descended upon Williamsburg with a near mutiny of troops posted there.

Many of Virginia's leaders believed Colonel Henry was a poor choice to command Virginia's troops. He had no previous military experience—his talents were much more political than military, they argued. When the Continental Congress selected several Virginians in 1776 to serve as generals in the Continental army, Colonel Henry was overlooked. He felt betrayed and insulted and resigned from the army in protest. When his troops learned about this, they too were upset and wanted to quit. Colonel Henry was still the most popular man in Virginia and his men felt he had been unfairly treated. They refused to follow orders and threatened to leave the army.

Colonel Henry's officers hosted a farewell dinner for him at the Raleigh Tavern before he left for home. James and John stood in two corners of the room, ready as always to assist if called upon. John was nearly in tears over how his hero had been treated by the Continental Congress and Virginia's own politicians.

The boys listened to officer after officer condemn the Convention and Committee of Safety, who they believed were behind Congress's decision to not promote Colonel Henry. Suddenly a messenger arrived from the regiment and handed a note to Colonel Henry. He rose to his feet and said, "Gentlemen, I thank you for this fine dinner, but we have work to do."

The officers followed Henry out of the Raleigh and hurried to camp where they found the soldiers of the 1st Regiment in an angry and rebellious mood. Most wanted to quit, but some threatened the Committee of Safety with harm.

"Soldiers, calm yourselves," Colonel Henry said as he stood before them. "Remember your duty. Thank you for this demonstration of your affection, but we must remain true to the fight. Much more is at stake than one man's pride. You must remember your duty, no matter your disappointment. Only Lord Dunmore will benefit if you turn from your duty now."

Colonel Henry assured them that although he was leaving the army, he was not leaving the fight.

"I shall continue the struggle by other means. But you must continue as you are. Stay true, stay true men. Stay true to Virginia and the righteous cause we fight for."

Henry talked with the troops all evening, moving amongst them and urging them to remain at their post. "Too much is at stake," he said over and over, "to abandon the cause now."

His efforts paid off. The disgruntled troops of the 1st Regiment remained in camp.

James and John were unaware of what happened that night in the 1st Virginia's camp. They learned about it later.

"Although I still find Mr. Henry a bit obnoxious at times," James said to his brother, "I do respect what he did with his troops the other night. A lesser man might have walked away or worse—encouraged the troops to mutiny."

John was pleased to hear James compliment Mr. Henry—he rarely ever did so.

By late March, the city was once again crowded with new soldiers and new officers, who, like those the previous fall, rushed about the city to obtain clothing, weapons, and gear for their men.

General Charles Lee arrived in Williamsburg at the end of March, generating great excitement. He was second in command in the Continental Army behind only General Washington, and many thought his prior experience in the British army made him the most skilled officer in the Continental army. He'd retired from the British army in 1773 and settled in Virginia, but when the fighting started in 1775, he offered his services and experience to Congress, who happily accepted.

Congress sent General Lee to Virginia in 1776 out of concern that the British planned to attack somewhere in the South. His stay in Williamsburg lasted just a month, during which he visited the Raleigh and Anderson's tavern several times.

Rebecca thought General Lee was a strange man, both in appearance and conduct. "He's so thin and excitable," she said to James and John one morning after General Lee dined at Anderson's tavern. "And I know he is supposed to be an expert on war, but all he talked about at dinner last night was dogs. He seems exceptionally fond of his dogs."

John came to General Lee's defense. "Well, they say that nobody—not even General Washington—is a better officer in our army. I doubt that, but am still glad he is here."

General Lee did not agree with the Committee of Safety's plan to post Virginia's new regiments in different parts of the colony to guard against the British. He wanted them concentrated closer to Williamsburg and issued orders for several regiments to march to the capital.

One thing that Williamsburg never seemed to be short of were officers. Some were posted in Williamsburg with their regiments, but others came to the capital without their men to conduct business on behalf of them. Most ate and often stayed overnight in the city's taverns, and this gave John an opportunity to converse with them. He peppered them with questions every chance he got.

"Do you think the redcoats will come here, sir? Will you be marching north? How long do you think the war will last? When will you finish off Lord Dunmore?" John had new questions every day and never hesitated to ask—despite the stern looks he received from his father.

James, as usual, preferred to listen rather than engage in conversation. At 13 years old, he looked like some of the younger soldiers in camp, and occasionally an officer asked him if he planned to join the army. "Yes, sir, I do," he always replied. "In three years, once I'm 16."

Most of the officers laughed at that. "Well, son, we should have this war won by then. You'll miss all the fun," they'd say.

James thought to himself how odd they should describe war as fun. He also noticed that it was usually the younger officers who said such things. The older ones—the ones with experience in the last war like Colonel Woodford and Colonel Mercer—never described war as fun.

Across the street, Rebecca, who was just a month away from her 12th birthday, also talked with the officers who dined and stayed at her father's tavern. Like John, she asked a lot of questions, but hers were different.

"Do you miss your family, sir? How long have you been away? Do you have any children, sir? You must miss them terribly. How long do you think the war will last?"

The older officers often complimented Rebecca for her kindness and compared her to their daughters at home. It made her sad to think of the officers and their families who missed each other so. She had always strongly believed that families belonged together.

General Lee learned at the beginning of May that a powerful British fleet had sailed to the Carolinas. He suspected that Charleston was their destination, so he ordered the 8th Virginia Regiment to join him and they marched south to help defend the city.

He left behind a Convention of delegates, Virginia's Fifth Convention, who gathered in the Capitol to consider a monumental issue, independence from Great Britain.

The talk in all the taverns now centered firmly on one topic—independence. There were a handful of men who argued against it, mostly on the grounds that the colonies were not ready for independence, but most insisted that it was time to break away from Great Britain.

James, John, and Rebecca all realized the significance of the issue. They met one afternoon before dinner to share what they overheard in the taverns. John, as usual, was in full support of independence. "We should have cast Britain off last year," he grumbled. James and Rebecca both agreed with him that it was probably time to separate from Britain.

"I think they've shown their real intensions to us," said James. "They want to crush and conquer us, so I think independence is really our only option."

Rebecca grudgingly agreed. "It's really their own fault," she said, referring to Parliament. "All they had to do was listen to us. We weren't unreasonable. *They* were. And still are! I think you're right, James. We no longer have a choice."

The Fifth Virginia Convention discussed this very topic for several days in the Capitol and then, on May 15th, the delegates voted unanimously for independence. The Convention instructed Virginia's delegates in the Continental Congress to propose that the American colonies become "free and independent States."

The Capitol

Chapter 12

God Save General Washington
1776

James, John, and Rebecca attended a grand celebration of the Convention's vote for independence the next day in Waller's Grove near the Capitol. The troops in the city were all paraded there, joined by the inhabitants of Williamsburg, and the Convention's resolution on independence was read aloud.

It was greeted with loud cheers and many toasts to American independence, the Continental Congress, and General Washington. The gentlemen of Williamsburg provided plenty of refreshments for each toast and everyone had a magnificent time.

In the evening the city was illuminated with torches and candles as the celebration continued. It was a joyous day, thought James, but one that meant more war—for he knew Britain would not let the colonies go without a fight.

Virginia's leaders wasted no time organizing a new government to replace the royal one they officially abandoned on May 15th. The Convention met every day to write a constitution for a new government, and James was fascinated with the nightly discussions he overheard at the Raleigh.

Mr. George Mason of Fairfax County intrigued James the most. He was insistent that a list of governing principles and rights be included in the new constitution. He argued that because the constitution would be the highest of all laws in Virginia, it must include a Declaration of Rights to protect the people from any possible abusive government in the future.

"Governments are made up of people," argued Mr. Mason, "and people are corruptible beings—especially when power is at hand. We must protect against the corrupting influence of power by enshrining these basic rights *into* our constitution."

James was very impressed by Mr. Mason. He particularly liked his argument—borrowed from the English philosopher John Locke and others—that all power derives from the people and that government power should be separated among branches to help protect against the abuse of this power.

James also agreed with Mr. Mason that a free press was essential to a free society by keeping the public informed of what their government was up to. *Perhaps, thought James, a republican form of government could survive if it followed such principles.*

After several weeks of debate, the Convention adopted a new constitution for Virginia and then elected Patrick Henry governor. John was thrilled with the news.

"Now he'll get back at those who abused him when he was with the army," he predicted.

That, of course, was not Governor Henry's intention. Even if he wanted revenge—and he did not—his new position as governor did not include the massive powers that the old royal governors had. If Governor Henry wanted to accomplish anything useful, he had to work *with* the new state General Assembly (which replaced the House of Burgesses), not against it. They had to share power, just as George Mason and others planned in the new state constitution.

While Williamsburg was abuzz with political talk, Governor Dunmore moved his small fleet of ships from Norfolk to an island in the Chesapeake Bay called Gwynn's Island. Tired of living onboard the ships,

Dunmore wanted to use the island as a new base of operation from which he would regain control of Virginia.

Virginian troops rushed to confront Dunmore and on July 9th, they bombarded his camp on Gwynn's Island with cannon fire. Rather than fight back, Dunmore—whose force was small and sickly, weakened by smallpox and other illnesses—fled back to his ships. He abandoned hundreds of dead and dying slaves, overcome by disease, who had joined him because of his promise of freedom. If they could not fight for him, they were of little use to Dunmore and better off dead, he believed.

Big John was unfortunately among those left on the island, struck down by smallpox. He had reached Lord Dunmore in Norfolk after the battle at Great Bridge and lived on one of Lord Dunmore's ships for months, like hundreds of other escaped slaves. He had never fought in a battle, much to his relief, but a week after they landed on Gwynn's Island, Big John came down with smallpox. Like many around him, he suffered miserably and died on Gwynn's Island.

Dunmore's defeat at Gwynn's Island was the final straw for him. He abandoned his efforts to regain Virginia and sailed for New York. Less than a week after the battle, news reached Williamsburg that the Continental Congress had voted for independence from Britain. James, John, and Rebecca were all proud that Mr. Jefferson, a Virginian, had written the document that announced it to the world—the Declaration of Independence.

The residents of Williamsburg celebrated the news from Philadelphia on July 25th. A copy of the Declaration of Independence was read aloud several times in the city to the cheers of the people. Musket and cannon salutes were fired after each reading.

James and Rebecca thought the Declaration a wonderful document. Mr. Jefferson explained in the document why the colonies had no choice but to separate from Great Britain. John was pleased with the Declaration too, but he found the musket and cannon fire more enjoyable.

In August, the 1st and 3rd Virginia Regiments marched north to New York to join General Washington in the defense of New York. The British had abandoned Boston in March and gone to Halifax, Nova Scotia to regroup. Everyone expected them to attack New York City so reinforcements were urgently called for. The 4th, 5th, and 6th Virginia Regiments marched for New York in

September. The 8th Virginia was still in South Carolina and Georgia and the 9th Virginia never left the eastern shore. The 2nd Virginia was still in Williamsburg, but most of its men left the unit when their enlistments expired in October, so the only complete regiment in Williamsburg in the fall of 1776 was the 7th Virginia Regiment.

A regiment of over 200 light dragoons (cavalry) also mustered in Williamsburg in the fall. Barracks behind the Governor's Palace were built to house both the dragoons and the infantry in the capital.

Governor Henry and his family lived in the palace and oversaw Virginia's military efforts in the war. John and Rebecca did not see Governor Henry as much as they used to. The responsibilities of government and war kept him busy at the Capitol and Palace. There were still plenty of guests at the taverns, however, and plenty of gossip.

The college reopened in the fall and James returned to continue his studies—this time in the college itself, instead of the grammar school. His friend, William Wormley, did not return, however. His family's loyalty to England and the King caused them to sail back to London late in the summer.

A few days after James returned to school, a disturbing report of a decisive American defeat on Long Island in New York spread through Williamsburg. John and Rebecca shared what they heard with each other on the porch of the Raleigh.

"Mr. Dixon said last night that he doubted our troops had reached the army yet, so they probably weren't in the battle," reported Rebecca.

"If anyone would know, he would," replied John. "The gazettes always get the news first. But I'm sure the Virginians were not there. If they had been, I bet the battle would have ended differently."

"I don't know," said Rebecca. "Mr. Dixon said there were 30,000 British and Hessian troops on Long Island eager to crush General Washington. He said there were so many British warships in New York Harbor, that it looked like a forest of masts. No one seems to believe General Washington can survive against such a force. I worry for him."

John didn't say so, but he worried for General Washington too.

More bad news arrived at the end of September. New York City had fallen to the British, but most of

Washington's army escaped and regrouped at White Plains, 35 miles north of the city.

The British commander, General William Howe, made his headquarters in New York City, but everyone expected his next target would be Philadelphia.

General Washington moved his troops into New Jersey to block the British and waited for General Howe to make his next move. It came in mid-November. Thousands of British troops crossed the Hudson River and marched into New Jersey, straight at General Washington. The vastly outnumbered Americans had no choice but to retreat, all the way across New Jersey. The reports that reached Williamsburg in early December painted a bleak picture for General Washington and his troops.

"They say General Washington's army has deserted him in New Jersey, and he doesn't have many men left," fretted Rebecca to John when they met on the porch of the Raleigh on December 3rd, James's 14th birthday.

"I've heard that he is retreating to Philadelphia to make a last stand there," said John. "But I don't understand how this could happen. We sent so many troops. Maybe the other states have quit the war?" he mused.

"I don't know what's happened, but it sounds pretty bad. Poor General Washington," Rebecca murmured.

Although the situation was indeed bleak for Washington's tiny army in December 1776, the few thousand troops who were still with him managed to cross the Delaware River on December 8, and temporarily escape from the British army. General Howe could find no boats to cross the river and continue his pursuit. General Washington had seized or destroyed them for miles up and down the river.

With no way to cross the Delaware River until it froze, General Howe ordered his troops into winter quarters. He posted 1,500 men in the town of Trenton on the Delaware River, and scattered the rest of his army in towns in New Jersey and New York to keep warm over the winter.

General Washington and his tiny army of just several thousand men remained in the field, freezing along the west bank of the Delaware River. They were temporarily safe, but in desperate shape. They needed winter clothes, food, and most importantly, more men—but few came forward. It seemed that most Americans considered independence a lost cause.

The American commander pleaded with Congress for help, but they had little to give. Even the troops still with Washington believed the war was lost and he confided to his brother in a letter a week before Christmas that, "unless something is done to reinforce our army, I fear the game is pretty near up."

Fearful that General Washington would be unable to stop the British from capturing Philadelphia when the Delaware River froze over, Congress fled the city. The American cause looked hopeless. But then, General Washington made a bold decision.

He learned a few days before Christmas that only 1,500 Hessian soldiers were posted across the Delaware River in Trenton. General Washington knew that time was running out and that he had to do something bold to boost American spirits. He decided on a daring plan to lead 2,400 men across the river in the middle of the night and attack the Hessians in Trenton at daybreak. He chose Christmas night to cross, and in order to surprise the Hessians, they crossed eleven miles upriver from Trenton.

This meant Washington's troops had to cross an ice choked river during a cold winter night and then march eleven miles in darkness to surprise and attack some of the best soldiers in the world. And to make matters worse, a snow storm hit while Washington and his men crossed the river and marched to Trenton.

Washington's troops suffered through the freezing night, but what was worse, most of their gunpowder was ruined by the storm. Still, Washington refused to turn back. "We shall use the bayonet," he declared when informed about the wet gunpowder. "I am resolved to take Trenton."

Fortunately for the Americans, the storm that made their crossing and march so difficult, caused the Hessians to let down their guard. No one would be so foolish as to be out in such a storm, their sentries thought, and many took shelter inside buildings rather than stand watch outdoors.

General Washington and his brave men suddenly appeared out of the blizzard and smashed the Hessians in Trenton on the morning of December 26th. Caught by surprise, the Hessians were unable to recover and most surrendered after a brief, disorganized fight. At the cost of just a handful of men, the Americans inflicted 100 casualties on the Hessians and captured over 900 prisoners.

A week later, Washington and his men did it again—winning a second battle against the British in Princeton, New Jersey.

Word of these victories electrified the patriots and their cause. Many had given up on independence, but Washington's bold actions revived their hopes. General Washington was toasted all over the country, but particularly in the taverns of Williamsburg. James, John, and Rebecca were thrilled by the news. Each was fond of General Washington and each was relieved that he was still safe with the army. They felt that the worst was over. Surely 1777 would be the year they won their independence.

James certainly hoped so, but John—who had just turned 13—foolishly hoped the war would last until he got a chance to fight.

Chapter 13

My God, Becca
1777

The renewed confidence James, John, and Rebecca felt for the war with Britain spread throughout the colonies. It did not, however, lead to the full recruitment of six new regiments approved by Virginia's government in the fall of 1776. It was a struggle at the start of 1777 to keep the original nine regiments fully manned. Sickness, desertion, and losses in combat the previous year reduced their numbers greatly. Recruiting over 4,000 additional men to fill the six new regiments proved nearly impossible.

The need for reinforcements for Washington's army in New Jersey meant that those who did enlist in the winter of 1777 were sent north as soon as possible.

Smallpox plagued both armies and despite his need for men, General Washington ordered that his troops—and all the new recruits—be inoculated for the disease. This was done by rubbing a small amount of pus from a person mildly sick with the disease—who was typically covered with pustules all over their body—into a small cut in the arm of the person being inoculated.

The inoculated person would typically develop smallpox within ten days of exposure, hopefully a mild case but sometimes it would become severe. They suffered through days of high fever, their body covered in pustules which eventually broke open, drained, and scabbed over. When the scabs fell off, the worst was over and the inoculated person, assuming they survived the fever—and most did—was immune from catching or, more importantly to General Washington, spreading the disease.

Mr. Southall declined to inoculate himself or his family, but Mr. Anderson did, and Rebecca, her parents, and little Hope suffered through an inoculation in February.

Mrs. Southall, who had survived a case of smallpox when she was a child, tended to the Andersons while they suffered through the month-long inoculation process.

John went to visit Rebecca as soon as she was recovered and able to have visitors. They sat on the front stoop of her tavern.

"It was awful, John," Rebecca said. "My head burned for days, and I could barely sleep I was so hot. And the scabs! They were everywhere. It was horrible!"

John grimaced at the description. "I'm glad you are well now," he said.

"Yes, thank you. Your mother was an angel to all of us. Please tell her so! We are all most grateful for her kindness. I pray you never have to go through it."

"I'm sorry it was so difficult, Becca. It sounds horrible. My mother says you were an ideal patient though," he grinned at her, "and very brave."

Rebecca smiled back at him.

John bowed his head, looking into the street. "Father says we should leave it to God to decide whether we catch the sickness or not. I guess I'm glad for that. I don't know if I could have endured it the way you did."

Rebecca understood John's concern—it was a horrible experience. But the doctor said that she and her family were now safe from the disease and that was at least some relief.

At the start of the new year the Southalls—overwhelmed by the demands of operating a tavern and raising a family that had grown to eight children—hired a tutor for John, his sisters, Frances, nine, and Elizabeth, seven, and brother William, six. His three youngest siblings, Anne, four, George, three, and Peyton, two, were still taught by their mother, but that task became much easier when Mr. Philip Pender arrived in January to tutor the older children.

Although John was no match for James in school, he did master the basics under his mother's care. His handwriting was bold and neat, with only an occasional misplaced or misspelled word. His understanding of mathematics was strong, and he had recently developed a greater interest in reading than in the past.

Mr. Pender was a young man in his early twenties. He was from Pennsylvania and thus, a stranger to some of the customs of Virginia. He despised slavery, thinking it inhumane to hold people as property, but he rarely discussed this belief, which was considered radical among most white Virginians.

Mr. Pender had attended the College of New Jersey in Princeton, and was a classmate of Henry Lee and James Madison, two fellow Virginians whose fathers believed the College of William and Mary was too rowdy for their sons. Both young Virginians were destined for great fame in the years to come.

The Southalls paid Mr. Pender £50 pounds a year to teach John and his siblings. He was provided a private bedchamber upstairs and dined with the family. Lessons occurred daily—except on Sunday—and covered a good part of each day. John primarily studied Latin and Greek, with some Natural Philosophy and Mathematics.

Mrs. Southall updated Rebecca on John's progress during her care for the Anderson family in February and March. "Would you like to come to the tavern and be instructed by Mr. Pender as well?" she inquired one day.

Rebecca was thrilled by the offer, unable to hide her excitement. "Oh, yes! Indeed, I would! You are so kind to ask."

Her parents were pleased by the offer as well and arranged to pay Mr. Pender £18 a year for Rebecca's lessons.

Surprisingly, and despite all the time she had spent with James and John over the last six years, Rebecca had spent very little time *in* the Raleigh. She now visited the tavern six days a week for her lessons and enjoyed it immensely.

In May, a delegation of Cherokee Indians came to Williamsburg to finalize a peace agreement with Governor Henry. A war with the Cherokee had broken out on

Virginia's frontier the previous year, but after some heavy fighting, a peace agreement was reached.

The Cherokee leaders met with Governor Henry in the palace and then performed a ceremonial dance on the palace green. Mr. Pender, who had a keen interest of the native peoples of North America, took Rebecca and John and his older siblings to watch.

"Watch their movements carefully," said Mr. Pender. "There is meaning in each one." Rebecca saw the grace of the dance but John, never one to appreciate dance, did not.

"Looks pretty easy to me," scoffed John, utterly unimpressed. "A lot easier than our dancing. But looks about as fun."

"It's ceremonial, Mr. Southall," replied Mr. Pender sharply. "They are paying respect to their ancestors."

"Well, I think it is fascinating," Rebecca said loudly. "The way they all move together *is* much like our dancing—just different steps and movements."

"Well said, Miss Anderson," replied Mr. Pender, pleased that at least one of his students appreciated the Cherokee dance.

"I don't see it," muttered John. "Just a lot of hopping and chanting."

Rebecca and Mr. Pender frowned at John. "Look at how they are dressed. Notice the ornaments they wear," Mr. Pender said.

Rebecca stood on her toes to get a better look. "What do they mean?"

"They represent their status with the Cherokee people," replied Mr. Pender. "These are likely some of their most important leaders."

When the ceremonial dance was over, Governor Henry stepped forward and offered the delegation some refreshments brought out from the palace.

As Mr. Pender and his students turned from the green to return home, John said, "Well, they certainly seemed friendly enough. I just hope they stay so."

"As do I, Mr. Southall, as do I," replied Mr. Pender.

Williamsburg was alarmed in August by reports of an enormous British fleet spotted in Chesapeake Bay. General Washington and his army had waited all year in New Jersey for General Howe and the British in New York to make a move against Philadelphia. The British commander wasted the entire summer, but finally sailed into Chesapeake Bay with a vast British fleet in late August.

Many in Williamsburg were at first fearful that Virginia was General Howe's target. Governor Henry was away from Williamsburg at his home in Scotchtown, so John Page, the Lieutenant Governor, called out the militia. 4,000 militia responded and were posted in Williamsburg, Yorktown, and Hampton to fend off a possible British attack. Both Captain Southall and Captain Anderson took the field with their companies.

General Howe was not interested in Virginia, however. Philadelphia was his objective, so his fleet sailed past Virginia all the way up Chesapeake Bay. Fifteen thousand British and Hessian troops landed at Head of Elk, Maryland, 50 miles southwest of Philadelphia in late August.

General Washington marched from New Jersey with the same number of troops to intercept the British and protect Philadelphia. One of the largest battles of the war was fought two weeks later along Brandywine Creek in Pennsylvania. It ended in an American defeat.

Two weeks later, Philadelphia fell to the British and a week after that, in early October, General Washington and his army were defeated in another battle outside of Philadelphia at a village called Germantown. Once again,

American hopes for victory and independence looked grim.

"Poor General Washington," said Rebecca, when she and John sat together on the porch of the Raleigh during a break in their lessons. "People are starting to criticize him."

"It's not his fault!" John yelled, angered at the thought that anyone would dare criticize General Washington. "He needs more men. He's fighting against *two* armies!"

John was referring to the fact that General Howe's army consisted of British and Hessian soldiers.

John threw his arms in the air, exasperated. "How can he be expected to win against *two* armies?"

Both Rebecca and John had heard criticisms of General Washington more and more in the taverns. But there had been some good news as well, so Rebecca tried to fix John's attention to that instead. "I heard Mr. Digges say that we stopped a British army in New York last month," she said.

The tension between John's brows softened. "Yes, I heard that too," he said. "They were trying to get to New York City from Canada and were stopped in the New York woods. I imagine they are limping back to Canada at this moment."

John's details were a little off, but the overall sentiment was correct. General John Burgoyne and 7,000 British and Hessian troops did indeed march from Canada into New York in the summer of 1777. They were joined by hundreds of Native American warriors and together they crushed American resistance on their way to Albany and the Hudson River.

Burgoyne's plan was to establish a line of British control from Canada to New York city along the Hudson River and Lake Champlain. If he could do that by marching to Albany, then the New England states would be cut off from the other states.

General Burgoyne was stopped, however, north of Albany by an American army commanded by General Horatio Gates. He was a retired British officer who had settled in Virginia before the war and his experience proved very useful to the Americans.

Two fierce and bloody battles were fought in September and early October above Albany, but General Burgoyne could not break through. He was forced to give up his march and return to Canada before the winter trapped him in the field.

John and Rebecca did not know this part when they talked on the porch of the Raleigh, but by the end of October they had learned of it and more. General Burgoyne and his entire army had surrendered near the village of Saratoga, New York on October 17th, 1777.

It was a tremendous American victory that, like Trenton and Princeton nearly a year earlier, boosted the morale of American patriots everywhere.

James, John, and Rebecca learned of the victory like everyone else—through the newspapers. Mr. Purdie's paper described the response in the city:

"The inhabitants illuminated their houses, and with the gentlemen of the General Assembly, spent a cheerful and agreeable evening."

The taverns, of course, were where many chose to enjoy the evening. And the talk around the gaming tables was all the same.

"*This* is the turning point!" everyone declared. "The King will surely give up the fight now."

Rebecca thought it a little odd that everyone seemed so happy. *Have they forgotten about Philadelphia and General Washington's army? What is to happen to them?* she wondered.

John had similar thoughts as he listened to the confident gentlemen celebrate at the Raleigh.

"Perhaps it is time that General Washington is replaced by General Gates," suggested one loud guest. "After all, Gates is a professional soldier while Washington…. Well," his voice trailed off.

"Excuse me, sir," John interjected. "But have you perhaps forgotten about Trenton and Princeton?"

The entire table looked up at John, and one of the gentlemen reached out to pat his shoulder. "Of course not Johnny. We remember Trenton and we all admire General Washington. But I'm afraid the task might be too great for him, son."

John was about to reply, but his father intervened and sent John to another room.

Those treacherous leeches, thought John. *So quick to compliment the General when things are well, but just as quick to desert him when things go badly.*

Governor Henry called for a day of Thanksgiving in mid-November in response to the victory at Saratoga. Virginians dutifully went to their churches and listened to speeches on a victory that was now within sight.

The following evening, a grand ball was held in the Capitol to celebrate the victory. Mr. Purdie's newspaper reported that:

> "All the ladies and gentlemen in this city, the military gentlemen and the strangers then in town all attended…Gaiety and good humor enlivened the ball, and socialness and jollity presided at the banquet."

Captain Southall and Captain Anderson both attended with their wives, and for the first time John and Rebecca joined them. So did James, who was excused from school for this special occasion.

Rebecca was both thrilled and terrified about her first ball. She had seen many at the tavern, but had never attended one and had certainly never danced at one. Her mother was equally excited and nervous for her daughter. She wanted the evening to be perfect for Rebecca and provided her with a new silk gown for the occasion. It was light blue with white lace and was the most beautiful gown Rebecca had ever seen. Mrs. Anderson gave her daughter a pearl necklace and matching pearl earrings to wear and they spent several hours preparing her hair. It was pulled back tight in the front and immaculately curled up in the back. Two long curls fell over her right shoulder and her mother placed a long white feather upon her head as a finishing touch. Mr. Anderson was speechless when he saw his daughter, his eyes glassy and smile wide.

Over in the Raleigh Tavern, James and John also prepared for their first ball. James wore a light blue linen coat with matching weskit and breeches and fine buckles on his shoes. John was dressed similarly, except his suit was a darker blue.

This was the first time that James, John, or Rebecca had ever been in the Capitol. The boys arrived before Rebecca and were awed when they entered the east wing entrance and climbed the stairs to the second floor. They made their way with their parents past a cluster of guests at the top of the stairs and entered a large room that held food and refreshments. Trays full of food and large bowls full of punch sat on several tables along the wall and a dozen round tables with chairs were scattered about the middle of the room to allow guests to sit and partake in the refreshments. Some played cards as they did so. Two well-dressed enslaved boys tended the tables and guests, hurrying up and down the stairs whenever the punch or food ran low.

A door led to a larger room where musicians played music. Chairs, and an occasional table, rested against the walls of this room, but the center was empty of all but guests, who stood in small groups and chatted while they waited for the dancing to begin.

Several other smaller rooms also held refreshments and tables to socialize around—but the main attraction that evening was to be dancing.

James and John and their parents were chatting with Dr. William Pasteur in the large room when Rebecca and her parents arrived.

The boys' backs were turned to the doorway when Rebecca entered behind her parents. John noticed her first and stared for a moment, then tapped James on the shoulder. James's eyes lit up when he saw Rebecca. She was an absolute vision of beauty.

Rebecca had an uncomfortable smile on her face, but when her eyes met James, her smile eased.

Both boys rushed toward her and bowed. "Miss Anderson," they said in unison. Rebecca curtsied and rewarded them with a smile in return.

"My God, Becca," John whispered as he leaned in close to her, "you look splendid tonight."

Rebecca laughed off the compliment and waved her fan to cool her blushing face.

James stood like a statue, still staring. He appeared to be in shock. Rebecca fixed her attention on him. "James, is something the matter?" James shook his head, seemingly in another world, but was totally unconvincing. Rebecca decided to ignore his odd behavior. She gave a small spin, her smile tight. "Well, how do you like my gown?"

James smiled and nodded. He tried to speak but felt like he had swallowed his tongue. He cleared his throat to try again. "Quite nice, quite nice," he muttered, and immediately felt foolish. *Nice?* he scolded himself, *that's the best you could do?* He shook his head, snapping out of his trance and feeling more in control of himself. He took Rebecca by the arm. "You have never been more beautiful, Becca. You are absolutely stunning."

A blush crept over Rebecca's cheeks. It was suddenly difficult to meet James's eyes. She fanned herself harder. "Why James, you and John look quite smart yourselves." She motioned toward the dance floor, trying to shift the attention off herself. "Isn't this grand?"

Just then a young man stepped forward, his hand outstretched toward Rebecca. "Miss Anderson, may I have the honor of the first dance with you?"

Rebecca did not know what to say. She wanted to dance with James and John, but they had not asked yet and her suitor deserved an answer. It came to her like a lightening bolt.

"Why, sir, I *am* sorry, but I promised the first dance to my father."

James stood there during this exchange condemning himself for not asking Rebecca to dance before this intruder walked up. He now seized the moment, leaning forward to ask, "Well then, may I have the dance after that?"

John immediately followed with, "and then I after James," sounding less like a question and more like a demand.

Rebecca smiled and nodded hastily. "Yes, yes, you may, you may."

The outmaneuvered young man frowned, clearly disappointed, but bowed to her. "Perhaps later in the evening then," he said as he turned away.

Governor Henry and his lovely young wife, 20-year-old Dorothea Dandridge, began the dance at 7 p.m. with a minuet. Governor Henry's first wife passed away in 1775, and although he was twenty years her senior, Miss Dandridge accepted his marriage proposal, and Henry's six children that came with it, in 1777.

Several couples followed the Governor and his wife on the dance floor, stepping their own minuets. There was a strict social order to the dance—it was *not* for everyone simultaneously. One's rank in society determined the order in which couples danced. It was stepped one couple at a time as a sort of showcase in front of everyone assembled. Minuets were not for the faint of heart or inexperienced dancers. Every move was judged by those watching—an audience who politely applauded when a couple finished, but who also noted every flaw that occurred in the dance.

The minuets were completed by 8:30 p.m. and it was then time for the country dances. These were the dances

Rebecca and the boys had practiced repeatedly with Mr. Fearson and she was eager to dance them now in this glorious setting.

Three musicians, two fiddlers and a flutist, played the dance tunes. One of the fiddlers called for the dancers to gather for the first dance.

It was tradition for the lady standing closest to the musicians to request a dance and the first dance was requested by Mrs. Bassett.

"May we have 'Well Hall?'" she asked.

The musicians nodded and began to play.

James and John did not dance the first dance, but Rebecca kept her word and danced with her father. She actually did better than he did—it had been a while since Mr. Anderson had taken to the dance floor. The boys beamed as Rebecca turned and moved about the set.

She is so elegant and graceful, thought James.

When the dance ended, he rushed to Rebecca and extended his hand.

"Will you now do me the honor, Miss Anderson?" he said as he took her hand, bowing slightly.

She smiled and looked at her father, who opened his arms as if to say, "you have my consent, dear."

They walked on the floor and danced a more complicated dance called "Dublin Bay." Rebecca remembered the movements, but James stumbled a few times and had to be corrected by her. When it ended, James's brows were nearly stitched together, his chest heavy with disappointment. But before he could speak, John was there, extending his hand to Rebecca for the next dance.

Rebecca knew how little John had enjoyed his dance lessons so she led him to the head of the dance line so that she could request the next dance. She chose "Hole in the Wall," the very dance they first attempted—so disastrously for John—six years earlier. *Surely he remembers this simple dance*, she hoped.

John did, and he danced it surprisingly well—much to the irritation of James who felt a twinge of jealousy. He wanted another dance with Rebecca, but several boys surrounded her once her dance with John ended. Embarrassed by all the attention, she accepted the offer of the closest boy to her and led him back to the dance set.

James realized that in order to be close to Rebecca again, he needed to take to the dance floor so that when the next dance ended, he could beat her other suitors and be the first to approach her.

James searched the room and saw Miss Hornsby, who had been one of his fellow dance students under Mr. Fearson. He strolled over to her and asked her to dance. Miss Hornsby startled a bit, surprised by the offer, but she smiled and accepted.

His plan worked perfectly. When the dance ended, James dashed over to ask Rebecca for the next dance. He did not even bother to nod goodbye to Miss Hornsby, who was left standing in a daze on the dance floor.

"Miss Anderson," he started, "I'm afraid my previous performance was not up to standard. I humbly ask that you grant me another chance."

Rebecca hesitated for a moment, looking over her shoulder and thinking of the others who wanted to dance. But then she looked back at James—his rigid posture, stiff smile, the tension was radiating off him. She gave him a tender smile and took his hand. "Of course."

They danced to "The Indian Queen" and this time, to his delight, James moved much more gracefully. "You're still an excellent dancer, James." Rebecca said when they finished.

His heart thumped loudly—the chatter in the room suddenly dulled by the sound of his own blood pulsing through his veins. His tongue felt swollen again, and before he could reply to her, she was whisked away by another suitor.

James did not get to monopolize her dance time like he wished. The other suitors had copied James's idea, joining the dance floor just to get closer and make the pounce quicker. James spent the remainder of the evening in the fray with the others, but his persistence paid off. By the end of the night, he was the person who had danced the most with Rebecca—and for that he was glad.

Poor John—who did not follow his brother's strategy—spent most of the evening in the adjacent room with the refreshments. He managed just one more dance with Rebecca near the end of the evening when she insisted that she needed something to eat and drink and had refused a dance with another.

She looks a bit pink, John thought as he watched her, slightly concerned.

It was true. Rebecca was flushed. Her eyes darted around the room in search of the mass of young gentlemen she could never seem to escape. *Have I finally evaded them?* she thought, her body relaxing at the prospect. But a second later, she spotted two on the move toward her. *Good lord, I cannot rest.* She gulped down some punch and stuffed a handful of candied walnuts into her mouth, chewing frantically.

"Becca, are you all—" John started, but she cut him off before he could finish.

"Mr. Southall, come, you must dance with me again," she said, taking his arm.

She led him back to the dance and they took their places. Once again, John did surprisingly well, and they laughed together when the dance was over.

It was nearly sunrise when the Southalls and Andersons retired for the night. As the guests poured out of the capitol, the brothers lost sight of Rebecca. They searched for her briefly, wanting to talk about the ball with her—how grand it had been, how exhilarating—but their father, who was quite red in the face from all the dancing and drink, prodded them toward home.

When the boys turned in for bed, they could think of little else but Rebecca—how beautiful she looked and how graceful she was. It was as if she had transformed into a fine lady overnight. Both boys were completely smitten with her.

In truth, there was no one Rebecca was fonder of than James and John, and her thoughts after the ball also dwelt on them. She cherished their friendship; it meant the world to her.

But something felt different after the ball. The formality of the evening had made the boys look more like young gentlemen than childhood friends. There had been an exciting tension throughout the night buzzing between them that had never existed before, and it both intrigued and worried her.

Rebecca did not dwell on this feeling, however. She was exhausted and needed to sleep. She resolved to think more about what happened at the ball tomorrow when she was rested.

It was late in the morning when the three met the next day on the Raleigh porch. They had all slept in.

"What a grand night," sighed Rebecca as she walked up the steps of the porch. "You two danced wonderfully."

The boys smiled and said over each other, "you were much better, Becca."

"Everyone wanted to dance with you," John said quickly, wanting to be the first to compliment her.

Rebecca, still unsure of how to respond to compliments, gave a shy smile and looked at her feet. "Well, it was a wonderful time and I think we all did fine for our first ball."

There was a strange and uncomfortable silence for a moment, as if each knew that things were different.

"I imagine," Rebecca started, the only one bold enough to break the silence, "the news of Saratoga will surely convince the King and Parliament to give up now."

"I hope so," said James quickly, thankful for the change of subject.

"They must see that they can never conquer us," added John. "They must be tired of this war, too."

"A lot of folks at the dance seemed to agree," said James. "They think the war will be over soon."

I certainly hope so, Rebecca thought. But in her heart, she didn't think it would be. Neither did General Washington and his tired troops encamped in Pennsylvania.

After a bloody fall and the loss of Philadelphia, General Washington and his troops faced a hard winter in the field at Valley Forge. The Continental Congress proclaimed its own day of thanks in mid-December. Joseph Plum Martin, a young soldier with Washington's army, recalled that to observe this special day, the troops were issued two ounces of rice and a teaspoon of vinegar. That was the extent of their extravagant feast.

Their adversaries, meanwhile, were comfortably sheltered in warm buildings for the winter in Philadelphia and New York. If any side was going to quit the war, thought Washington's men, it sure didn't look like it would be the enemy.

General Washington and his army knew that more struggle lay ahead. But for James, John, Rebecca, and many others, it was easier to hope that the war was almost over—even if it wasn't.

There were, of course, many reasons to hope for the war's end. But the main reason for Rebecca was that time was running out for her dearest friends. John would turn 14 and James 15 in December, which meant that the pressure for them to join the fight would grow stronger. Militia service was required in Virginia at age 16, but she knew there were boys younger than that in both the militia and continental army.

She listened as the brothers talked amongst themselves—now thoroughly engaged in a conversation about General Washington—and her stomach clenched, her heart suddenly heavy. *This dreadful war has to end soon,* she prayed, *else I could lose the boys to it.*

Heritage Books by Michael Cecere:

*A Brave, Active, and Intrepid Soldier:
Lieutenant Colonel Richard Campbell
of the Virginia Continental Line*

*A Good and Valuable Officer:
Daniel Morgan in the Revolutionary War*

*A Universal Appearance of War:
The Revolutionary War in Virginia, 1775–1781*

*An Officer of Very Extraordinary Merit:
Charles Porterfield and the American War for Independence, 1775–1780*

Captain Thomas Posey and the 7th Virginia Regiment

*Cast Off the British Yoke:
The Old Dominion and American Independence, 1763–1776*

*Great Things are Expected from the Virginians:
Virginia in the American Revolution*

*He Fell a Cheerful Sacrifice to His Country's Glorious Cause:
General William Woodford of Virginia, Revolutionary War Patriot*

*In This Time of Extreme Danger:
Northern Virginia in the American Revolution*

*Second to No Man but the Commander in Chief:
Hugh Mercer, American Patriot*

*They Are Indeed a Very Useful Corps:
American Riflemen in the Revolutionary War*

*They Behaved Like Soldiers:
Captain John Chilton and the Third Virginia Regiment, 1775–1778*

*To Hazard Our Own Security:
Maine's Role in the American Revolution*

Virginia's Continentals, 1775–1778: Volume One

Virginia's Continentals, 1778–1783: Volume Two

*Wedded to My Sword:
The Revolutionary War Service of Light Horse Harry Lee*

*Williamsburg at War:
Virginia's Colonial Capital in the Revolutionary War*

Witness to Revolution: Growing Up in Williamsburg During the American Revolution
Michael and Jennifer Cecere

Printed in the USA
CPSIA information can be obtained
at www.ICGtesting.com
JSHW011915270723
45408JS00001B/6

9 780788 429750